THE
PROGRAM

www.mascotbooks.com

The Program

For more information, please contact:
Mascot Books, an imprint of Amplify Publishing Group
620 Herndon Parkway, Suite 320
Herndon, VA 20170
info@mascotbooks.com

Library of Congress Control Number: 2021914772

CPSIA Code: PRV0422A
ISBN-13: 978-1-63755-162-2

Printed in the United States

For my wife, Sandra, the only one who believed in me.

THE
PROGRAM

A NOVEL

CHRISTOPHER GRAHAM

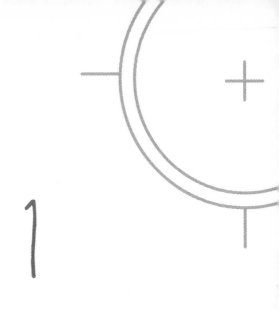

1

> *Beware that, when fighting monsters, you yourself do not*
> *become a monster . . . for when you gaze long into the*
> *abyss. The abyss gazes also into you.*
> *—Friedrich W. Nietzsche*

If this endeavor was ever going to fail, the betrayal was always going to come from within. And more than likely, the challenge was to be from a most unexpected place.

Saul Vitetto reached out to put his hand on Xantha's shoulder to give both comfort and guidance. Saul had been there from the beginning, and he was also the most loyal of soldiers: a true believer in every sense. And he had reason to be.

"This was never going to end well for him, ma'am," Saul began. "You and I both knew this." He was careful to make this last point so as not to disrespect the process in front of them. "We should have known from the beginning that he wouldn't have the stomach for this."

Agent Xantha Grasso, called X by some, nodded in agreement, maintaining her stony glare. "No one sees what I see," she said. "No one seems to know what I know"—she turned to look Saul in the eye—"because no one has the guts to see the truth."

She thought back to just how much she had accomplished in this particular effort and winced in pain at what she was being forced to do next. It seemed an eternity ago that her mission had begun to stabilize from something so hopelessly chaotic into something so remarkably formulaic and sound under her steady hand. All Xantha needed to do was open the thick metal door that led to her prisoner, and she could even out this last wave of dissent. Like Jesus when he calmed the storm, Xantha was wholeheartedly prepared to ask any and all who dared to question her motives, "Why are you so afraid? Do you still have no faith?"

With the dossier of the man who waited inside in her hands—a man she had trusted for so very long—she took one more moment to savor the flavor of her conquest while simultaneously bemoaning her inevitable loss. And to lament how it had ever come to this.

Saul confirmed what Xantha was thinking.

"Always remember, ma'am . . . and this is important. Whatever happens next, he did this to himself." He reiterated for effect, "He knew what he was signing up for, and he knew there was no way out but this one."

That helped a little, she thought. And as Grasso stood upon the precipice of her vengeance . . . she reveled in it. She took one more deep breath, reached for the door, and pulled it open, leaving Saul outside to stand guard. "No one leaves this room without my personal authority," she reminded Saul. "If this goes sideways, you know what to do."

Saul eyeballed the two "in case of emergency"-type plungers affixed to the wall above her head. Saul's eyes dropped from that LRT device (the "Last Resort Tactical Weapons" apparatus, which he helped create) to Xantha's eyes, and they both nodded in agreement. She slammed the door shut behind her and walked across the cold converted cafeteria that had become her interrogation room. This room held many memories for her, most of them satisfying.

She put her odds at one chance in three that this current memory was going to fall into that category. Or maybe she would have no memory of it at all. She truly did not know.

The room was poorly lit, with a metal table in its center and a bright lamp over it. There were no windows. Of course. No one was going to ever know what went on in this room. Ever. At the very least, Saul was standing outside the door to guarantee this, one way or another.

Thomas Duphrane, her longtime friend and a founding member, sat at a metal table facing her. His right hand was chained to it, and he was still wearing the olive double-breasted suit that he was wearing at the moment of his betrayal, she took note of how calm he appeared to be. Unshaven but handsome, Thomas gently slouched, as his mop of salt-and-pepper hair appeared mussed yet dignified. He seemed resigned to his fate, almost welcoming it. *In his mind*, she thought, *he* must *know it's over, and he also must know, in particular, what was coming next.*

Grasso, in her black pantsuit uniform, dark hair, and fair complexion, strolled over to her chair at the table and sat down. She lifted the file in her hand, placed it on the table, and slid it toward her handcuffed nemesis.

Without even looking at it, Thomas shoved the file off the table, maintaining his gaze upon Xantha's face. "I know what that file says."

Xantha drew a breath that reeked of disappointment and then began:

"I do not believe that I can ever express to you the level of my absolute disappointment in you, and I am entirely confident with that statement." Grasso had been known to speak in this manner throughout her career: to the point, calm, and with little-to-no room for discussion.

Thomas appeared unmoved by this display and actually managed a smirk.

Grasso continued. "We're trying very hard, those of us within The Program, to understand why it is that you have decided to betray us. Whatever the reason, we're not going to allow you to damage what we've built any longer." Grasso waited a beat and then sustained her assault. "There are several conclusions that you can draw from your traitorous actions tonight." Agent Grasso leaned in for effect. "First of all, and this is extremely important. You're going into The Program . . . tonight."

Thomas thought about this for a moment and then shot back. "I'm way past that, Xantha. You can't scare me with that statement anymore. You *must* know this. Your Program is an absolute abomination—perverted and cruel—and I am forever sorry that I was any part of it," Thomas continued without raising his voice. Pausing for effect, Thomas finished his thought. "And it's going to take more than that to keep you safe from whatever is coming next."

Agent Grasso, hesitating to be sure Thomas was finished, went on as if Thomas had not even spoken. "After you go in, I will go home, eat some dinner, take a shower, find Sandra . . . and put her in The Program too." Grasso remained calm and slowly shook her head.

"You see, Thomas?" Grasso continued, "Other people, people *you* care about, are going be injured and erased as a consequence of what you've tried to do to this Program. My Program. People you never ever thought about are now front and center and in mortal danger . . . people like Sandra. People like . . . your father."

Thomas was stone-faced. "Sandra knew the risks of loving me . . . " Thomas offered without hesitation. "She has been loved deeply by me, if only for a short while, and that is more than most could ever ask or want." Thomas gave Xantha the proverbial relationship needle. "Or maybe you have no idea what I'm talking about." Then Thomas continued, "And as for my father, well, he's dying of prostate cancer, so you're too late for him."

"We'll see . . . " said Grasso. Xantha was silent for a moment, marveling at the fact that this was where they were. Then she smirked a bit, and asked, "You saw your father?"

"Last night, actually," Thomas replied. "He put me back on the right path."

"Well, that's his job, isn't it?" Xantha said.

Thomas grinned. "It is, to be sure. Even on his deathbed, my dad is still saving souls."

Xantha nodded, "Good. Good for him. The man has that 'character of his conviction' thing that I love about passionate people." Xantha then turned her attention back to the task at hand.

"You know something, Thomas?" she continued. "It is not I who has betrayed us, but you. I have made no bones at all as to what I wholly intended and expected The Program to be. And I found an audience who was ready, willing, and able to listen—and to act." Grasso raised her voice. "I have given this nation, this government, these people, and these citizens *exactly* what they had asked for and, ultimately, legislated for." She pushed herself toward her former friend, getting a bit in his face. "I am the loyal soldier, while you are traitor."

Thomas silently smirked, "I'm sorry you feel that way. Giving people what they want doesn't always make you right." He continued, saying calmly, "History will remember my name, and what is happening here today."

Grasso returned to her chair and sat down. "No . . . they will forget."

Thomas, sensing that another opportunity may not reveal itself, began to make his case. "Xantha, for what it's worth, this Program was nothing more than a radical idea gone awry. The Program is *wrong*. I know that now. It is a horrible perversion, and it is so far away from what was intended. I am forever stained by it." Thomas went on, "You almost made me lose my soul when you brought me on board with this. Thank God I was able to right that ship before it sank. And would you like to know something else?" Thomas paused, waiting on Xantha.

Xantha opened her hands, egging Thomas on.

Thomas continued, "I don't even remember who I was before you and this Program sunk your claws into me." Thomas shook his head in disbelief. "I don't know what I was thinking, throwing my hat into the ring with you. This thing is beyond evil. I just didn't see that before it was too late."

"The Program is evil only to those who don't understand it," Grasso answered quickly.

"On the contrary, this Program is evil to those who *do* understand it," Thomas shot back. "I know that Saul is on the other side of that door, willing to do *anything* to keep this Program alive. Willing to kill me. Committed to killing *you* if you ask him to." Thomas sighed. "It's taken me a long time to get to this point. I know now what a monster I have become. I know now what horrible things I am capable of. Because of you."

"Because of *me*?" Xantha shot back. "Right. You had nothing at all to do with this . . . I would love to hear how I somehow forced you to come with me on this." Xantha shook her head incredulously. She sat back in her chair, placed her hand below her nose on her own face, and smiled quietly. "Go ahead, Thomas. Please, regale me with how The Program did nothing but make your life one for the ages, if you had only the courage to be loyal."

Thomas nodded, "Yes, I'll admit. In the beginning, one could argue I was a true believer. But as the layers of this . . . disgrace . . . were being pulled back, as the truth was slowly being revealed as to what this either was becoming or maybe *was* in the first place, it became something . . . unholy."

Grasso added, "Or . . . it became what it was always destined to be."

Thomas continued. "I saw the news last night. This Program is starting to spin out of control, isn't it? It's becoming something that you are going to have a hard time getting your hands around, I can tell. And soon, The Program is going to grow past you, and then . . . they'll take it away, either by force or by some sort of wicked legislation. Rest assured." And then Thomas leaned in, "And I don't care *what* the president said to you. Your days are numbered. I hope you're ready for that."

Thomas then spoke from a position of intellectual history. "We, as a society, have been moving away from what we thought was right, and toward something that we know is wrong. We do this willingly and without remorse. We saw this and did nothing. And we are now suffering the consequences of that choice. Right here. Right now." Then Thomas went one step further. "You and your cronies have always been like cockroaches. Constantly lurking in the shadows, protected by darkness. Well, the light is turned on now, and I can see that you're going to be scrambling for the dark. And I'm just trying to make sure you get stepped on."

A hint of rage began to boil up as Grasso mustered the strength to answer Thomas's claim.

"Tommy . . . what did you think this was? I mean, I plucked you straight out of the choir. When I first met you, you were this college student who had these radical ideas . . . ideas that I streamlined for you. I took what you saw about society and made it operational. You were all *for* The Program. And, by the way, for all the right reasons. I know that you saw what I saw. In every step of this process, and in the faces of those who were innocent victims, we were *desperate* to help them! And if we had to do addition by subtraction, then so be it." Xantha took a breath, and then continued. "This is what perplexes me about this moment right now, and I simply do not understand you." She leaned in, "There is absolutely no way that you could have *possibly* looked at what The Program was, what it was becoming, and not see it for what it is . . . "

Grasso paused, then finished, as she whispered . . .

"A *solution* . . . "

Grasso hesitated, then asked the question that seemed cheap, but still *had* to be asked. "Why? Why did you insist on doing this?"

Tommy had a simple, straight answer. "Math. A simple 'actuarial analysis.' Too many people getting hurt for too little payoff. You say that we were protecting innocent people? That might be true. But I feel like we were acting as judge, jury, and executioner this whole time, and that *never* leads anywhere good." Thomas drew a breath and sat back in his chair. "I've made my peace with the consequences of my actions here . . . Sandra too. I know my life has been forfeit for quite some time now, but there was no way I could stand by and allow this to continue."

Xantha sat back in her chair, an incredulous look passing over her face. "I mean, Jesus, Tommy . . . you picked our first subjects. These were *your* subjects."

Tommy began to tear up and answered back, a wounded look on his face. "I'm more than aware of the role I have played in this monstrosity."

"Then what are we even talking about?" Grasso asked, exasperated. "You can't be onboard, have an attack of self-righteousness, and then jump off-board. You *know* that's not how this thing works . . . you could have talked to me."

"And what would you have said? 'It's fine, Tommy, just go on with your life without us.' No. You would have never let that happen. I am forever stained—and my soul mutilated—by this Program. I won't do this anymore." Finishing his thought, Tommy added, "I always knew that I was in for a penny, in for a pound." Then Tommy made a simple point. "Xantha, we're killing people. Innocent people."

Xantha grinned in disbelief. "Innocent, Tommy? Innocent

of what?" Grasso fell back in her chair and threw up her hands, the magnitude of this moment beginning to wash over her. "I mean . . . what am I supposed to do here?" Grasso asked, "Because, no matter what I do next, this gives me no joy."

Tommy answered for her, "I'll tell what you should do. You had better kill me, X. Because if you don't, I'm going to blow this whole thing wide open." Tommy continued, "You have worked too hard to get what you want, don't let your conscience give you pause now. You've taken that out of the equation years ago." He leaned in, "If you let me live, this whole thing is *over*. You know it, and I know it." Tommy hesitated and then continued, "And I'm not the only one who feels this way. If I had to make this decision and I were you, I would kill me twice."

"You know, you're just making this easier for me . . . " Xantha explained.

"Well," Thomas finished, "I aim to please."

"It didn't have to be this way . . . " Grasso continued.

"You already told me that. Let's get this over with already," Thomas retorted. "My soul is prepared, how's yours?"

Agent Grasso exhaled the way a person does when they are about to do something that they know they're going to regret. "Tommy," she started, "Tommy, I'm about to give you a privilege that, quite frankly, I feel that you have earned . . . "

She reached into her jacket and produced a .38 pistol. Laying the piece on the table, Grasso explained, "Because of your service to this cause, and the fact that you have been with us since the beginning, I will extend you the courtesy of ending your time in The Program with dignity and honor."

She slid the weapon toward her prisoner. "Within this tool lies one bullet. Place the weapon next to your temple, pull the trigger, and you will honorably enter your rebirth."

She looked at the guards and said, "Take those cuffs off." Her guards gave her the look of resistance. "Just do it, and lower your weapons . . . "

A burly guard cautiously walked over the prisoner, uncuffed Tommy's hand, and returned to his post, weapon down.

Tommy smirked and then fumbled at the weapon, thinking it was a trick. "I know what you're trying to do. I reach for the weapon, and these boys behind me put me down."

Grasso shook her head. "No. They have orders to let this play out no matter what happens." To reinforce this, she yelled out, "Is that understood gentlemen? On my authority and on my responsibility, do not draw down on this man . . . " she waited a moment, then looked at Tommy, "or on me."

She received the required "Yes, sir" response she was looking for, then tilted her head toward Tommy. "See? No tricks . . . just choices."

Tommy eyeballed the weapon on the table and started to think it through. He knew this might still be a trick, but then again, it might not be. Was this one last loyalty lesson? Was this some power play just for show? There was no way that he was walking out of here alive. Thomas knew that. But maybe he could perform one last heroic act. He tongued his left-side molar, secretly releasing a cyanide capsule that gently clicked against his teeth, and then was still. One last mission. One last-gasp effort to finally bring it all crashing down.

Tommy reached for the weapon lightning fast before he

could change his mind and jumped to his feet. He pointed the gun at Grasso's head. "One bullet? You should have known I was never going to make this *easy* for you. You should have known I don't care what happens to me." He fingered the trigger and took off the safety. "And you should have thought about how I was going to *use* that bullet . . . I'm not as honorable as I used to be . . . "

Grasso, calmly and quietly, smiled and said, "That much is certain. Now don't disappoint me."

Thomas said one last thing, and it was done. "You know something Xantha? The one who wins the sword fight is the one who's not afraid to die . . . " There was a click of something that was hitting his teeth, and then a crack and a crunch.

Xantha curled her mouth in a knowing way. And then it was over.

Her prisoner fired, and the rigged gun exploded toward his face, destroying most of his head in a ghoulish bloody mess. As her now twice dead prisoner fell to the floor, Grasso stood, grabbed her files, and flipped them toward the dead body.

"Goodbye . . . Agent Thomas Duphrane . . ." Then she added, "Make sure that file goes in there with him."

Then, Agent Grasso said something that was peculiar for her, but poignant nonetheless. She said, as she rose from her chair, moved around the table, and stood over the remains of her friend: "I have decided to forgive you. And not for any other reason except that, try as you might, you did not wound me." And then she got down on one knee and whispered, "But it was a valiant effort, and I applaud your conviction. I always said that if I can have honesty, then it is easier to overlook mistakes."

Grasso took one last look at the mess Agent Duphrane had made of himself and moved toward the door. "Saul! Authorization four-seven Alpha Tango!" The door buzzed, and then unlocked from the other side. And she left, erasing someone that she had wildly misread, but also someone whom she owed an enormous amount.

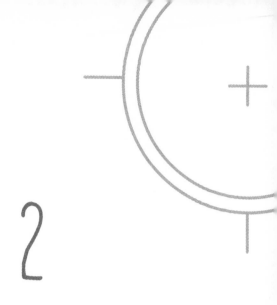

2

> *The happiness of a country does not depend, absolutely,*
> *upon its poverty or its riches . . . but upon the rapidity*
> *with which it is increasing, upon the degree in which the*
> *yearly increase of food approaches to the yearly increase*
> *of an unrestricted population.*
> —*Thomas Robert Malthus*

"There are too many people." That was a phrase that many had heard for a long period of time. "All of the world's problems would become less if we just eliminated some people." Comedians and politicians alike professed the unmitigated truth that the amount of people that were on Earth was in direct proportion to the pain, misery, despair, hunger, crime, and financial well-being of the said planet. This seemed to be a fact, and it was undisputed.

The Cellular Reorganization Program, or CRP, had always been around, lurking inside the thoughts and minds of even the most liberal thinkers of the time. The Program had evolved organically enough. From the simplest of ideas, borne out of emotion and anger, the CRP had become the overriding policy of the current administration. Employing thousands of citizens and enduring thousands of challenges, the CRP was near to becoming the law of the land.

But, just like many things, The Program began so innocently enough that if one were not looking, they would have missed it. Just like many things, it was immediately deemed wrong. But as it was without consequence, it went uncorrected. Because, although the genesis of The Program was immoral, it catered to the basest elements of the human condition.

For thousands of years, humanity had moved closer to, and farther away, from what it might look like to be decent. Left to their own devices, humanity would, quite simply, never survive. Humans are constantly forgetting several critical elements of their own existence. Mainly, that they are still part of the animal kingdom. Humans are still beholden to the simplest of emotion and instinct. Whether it be the idea that the acquisition of wealth is the driving force of its existence, or whether adhering to the Golden Rule is absolutely the way to live, humanity seems to be in a constant state of eternal struggle mitigating these two extremes.

Indeed, one can easily argue that the answer lies somewhere in between, and that in itself is entirely the problem. Governments are put in place to make these decisions for us, and when they falter and lose their moral compass, the consequences of that failure are absolutely devastating.

Civilization is much more fragile than it appears to be to the naked eye. One false move, and it can all come crashing down. Indeed, it *has* all come crashing down.

History has shown, time and time again, how close humanity has been to essentially being forced to start all over. The Program is a product of this eternal frustration. What is society to do with people who continue to make what one might argue is the *wrong decision*? At what point are people, who society feels should know better, to be given up on? And how long are those who *do* play by the rules going to carry those who willfully *don't*?

Xantha Grasso considered herself a trailblazer: a moral pioneer. While everyone and their mothers had been advocating what she had been imagining for decades, Grasso had the gumption to bravely move forward with something that *she* thought everyone wanted. The idea had been buried inside of her since her senior year in high school, and it was a poignant moment indeed.

Her biology class had taken up the task of raising twenty-four chicks from the incubation period all the way to their individual hatchings. It was a delicate, grueling process that took weeks to complete. But Xantha's teacher noticed how intense Xantha's attention was to the entire process. Within days, Mr. Bajor had placed Xantha in charge of the entire program. Xantha was given special permission to leave some of her other classes early and to stay after school unsupervised since she could drive herself whenever she wished.

Xantha adjusted the lights, regulated the amount of hay, and covered eggs that she felt were not receiving enough warmth. Xantha was doing a spectacular job, and when the day came when the eggs began to hatch, she encouraged each egg personally to release their chicks. One by one, and sometimes two or three at a time, the eggs hatched.

Wearing gloves and a mask (at this point, she was fancying herself as not a nurse but a doctor), Xantha not only made certain that every egg was cared for, but also delegated out to the other class members (there were eleven other students) certain important tasks once the chicks appeared.

"Gently rub this one, she's cold. Clean under this one's wings. This one is smaller than the rest—separate it and get it some food and water."

She ordered the students to perform these tasks for the next hour and, in the end, every chick had successfully hatched. There were twenty-four specimens, and now, there were twenty-four chicks. There were ten aquarium cases placed atop ten lab desks, with two set aside for the special chicks, such as the ones who appeared underdeveloped, malnourished, or just plain different. There were three of these chicks that fit into this category, and the rest were placed into all the other remaining aquarium cases. The room was alive with the gentle chirping of newborn chicks, and they were all fed, watered, and bedded down for the night. It was 2:30 p.m., and it was a Wednesday.

During the night, some chicks got better and some got worse. Xantha came in early to check on them all and found that the three that had been segregated had not improved. In fact, they had all grown worse. *And* . . . two of the others had suffered injuries in the overnight, so now there were five chicks that were injured or imperfect. Slowly, the rest of the students filed in, and, interestingly, they all gravitated to the healthy chicks. Xantha still stood over the five, seemingly becoming convinced of what to do next.

Xantha Grasso never did anything without thinking it through in its entirety. Formulaic, reasoned, and without emotion seemed to be the scientific method that Xantha had built for herself. Indeed, her instructor Mr. Bajor himself, a former government worker in the Biological Engineering division of the CIA (among other divisions), had begun to take notice. The fact that Mr. Bajor had been a former CIA agent was widely known within the school (and had given him a bit of a rock star/cult status). But what *wasn't* known was that the CIA accepted Bajor's resignation under the condition that he would constantly be on the lookout for students whom he thought would be potential agents. Bajor had yet to even sniff a student who would have been an acceptable candidate at this point. But Xantha Grasso intrigued him, and he began to document her progress as a student . . . just in case.

Xantha continued to peer into her aquarium that housed her personal "Island of Misfit Toys" and continued to reason out what to do next with the group. She performed certain physical tests on them, such as trying to equate their strength and agility. She tested their senses as well and watched how well they fed themselves and how well they drank their water. All five were performing poorly, and she documented their lack of progress and performance in her biology journal.

While Xantha continued to observe the chicks that were, in many ways, substandard, the entire class continued to fawn over the nineteen chicks that were typical. Mr. Bajor walked over to Xantha and asked her what she thought.

"These chicks are substandard," she began. "I project that caring for them is going to take over 25 percent of our time. In addition, taking care of these five is going to jeopardize the health and well-being of the remaining chicks."

Bajor nodded in both agreement and astonishment at Xantha's assessment. "What do you propose, Xanny?"

Xantha, continuing to look into the *case of five*, wondered aloud. "I have an idea . . . " Then, stroking her chin, she said, "We'll set it as a last resort," and walked away, still deep in thought.

Mr. Bajor marveled at Xantha's cool, analytical mind, leaving the solution up to her for now, and went back to his desk. Xantha went over to the other students, quietly advising them, guiding them, and instructing them as to the care of the nineteen healthy chicks, all the while crunching data in her mind as to what to do with the case of five. The bell rang, and the students slowly dispersed to their next classes, including Xantha, who went on with her day.

Later that day, when school was about to let out, Xantha returned to Mr. Bajor's classroom to check on her case of five chicks. The room was dark, lit only with the lamps that were warming the chicks in each glass cage. Mr. Bajor was at his desk in the back of the room, and he saw when Xantha came in. He quietly moved to Xantha's side as she continued to look in on her wounded chicks.

"You know, Xanny. I used to work for the CIA."

Xantha quietly rolled her eyes. *Yes*, she thought, *you tell us all the time*.

Mr. Bajor continued. "The Agency used to posit several scenarios that *they* would consider 'no win scenarios,' just for the purpose of observing how we would all react."

Xantha kept looking at her chicks but was also intently listening to Mr. Bajor's story.

"Many of these circumstances involved questions that weren't based in any sort of reality, but they *were* based in a type of moral equation.

"Once, I was tasked with the rescuing of two separate groups of four operatives that were hopelessly pinned down by enemy fire. I was told that I absolutely *had* to rescue both groups, and I only had a limited amount of time and weaponry that made the mission almost impossible. I laid out my plan and submitted it to my handler. Each time I was shot down, I kept crunching the numbers, trying in vain to rescue each operative, just as I was instructed . . .

"Then, I looked to my handler, and I realized the truth. I said, 'I can't save them all, so I'm choosing to save these four.' And I pointed out why this one and not that one and what is gained and lost with each. And, most importantly, how each operative knew the price of being a part of the CIA . . ."

Then, Mr. Bajor leaned in.

"And I *made* my choice and moved on with my life." He waited a moment and then asked Xantha, "Have *you* made *your* choice?"

Xantha's eyes lit up for a moment, and she acted. Reaching into the glass aquarium, she picked up the most wounded chick that was the least likely to survive. The chick chirped a few times, then it sat in her hand. This particular chick had an eye that had clouded up, had one wing that had not formed at all, and was born with a broken webbed foot that would never heal correctly.

Xantha closed her free hand around her bottom hand, and looked at Mr. Bajor.

"I feel as though it is best for all involved that this chick is removed from the equation before us."

Mr. Bajor placed a towel over the top of her hands.

"For the greater good, Xantha."

Mr. Bajor nodded and turned his back. Xantha, in one motion, crushed the chick in her hands, then quickly whipped the towel around to catch any blood or debris that would escape. There was none. There was only the slight squeak of the crumpled chick, and then silence. Xantha wiped her hands, which were remarkably clean, tied off the towel, and placed it in the large garbage can next to the sink.

Mr. Bajor turned back and said, "You're a natural, Xanny. Except, there was the slightest peep from the subject that you eliminated." Mr. Bajor reached into the glass cage and picked out another subject. "Get that towel and place it over this chick."

Xantha did. Then Mr. Bajor explained.

"Try to find the vulnerable part of the throat with your fingers. Wait until you can measure the breathing. Then, on the exhale . . . " And Mr. Bajor made his move. All they each heard was a slight crunch, then nothing. He was able to wrap the towel, tie it off, and dispose of it in one motion.

Xantha seemed to look at Mr. Bajor in awe, which caused him to say, "Don't worry, we'll work on it. You'll get there."

They both picked up two more of the flawed chicks. Each placed the chicks in their hands and covered their hands with a towel. Looking each other in the eye, they both quietly counted "one, two, three . . . " and then successfully crushed their victims.

In silence. No noise at all. Excellent.

Only one chick remained, and Xantha had an idea. She gently picked up the chick and walked it over to the sink. She filled the sink up, then looked at Mr. Bajor for confirmation.

Mr. Bajor put up his hands as if to say, "Hey, this is your thing. Go for it."

Xantha cupped the chick in her hands and dunked it into the water, holding it there so that it would drown. The chick squirmed, flapped its tiny wings, and splashed water on Xantha's face and clothes. After about thirty seconds, movement stopped, and the chick was limp in the water. Xantha pulled the waterlogged chick out of the sink, and it was soft, wet, and mushy in her hands. She grabbed a towel, wrapped it up, and dropped it into the trash.

She shook her hands to release the water off of them, and looked at Mr. Bajor.

"Okay. That wasn't the best way to do that."

Mr. Bajor agreed. "I was going to mention to you that elimination using water is always an aggressive choice in every way. But then I thought, 'Let's let Xanny find out for herself.'"

"Okay . . . that method is out."

They both turned to look at their remaining healthy chicks, and a certain level of pride washed over both of them. Unconsciously nodding to each other, they both thought, *Yeah, okay, this works* and moved separately toward the nineteen chicks that were left. They inspected all nineteen and concluded that nothing more remained to be done.

"So," Mr. Bajor began, "what are we going to tell the other students about the five chicks that we took care of?"

Xantha smirked and said, "Tell them the chicks went to a farm upstate. That's what everyone says when they euthanize the family dog, why not just say that?"

Mr. Bajor smiled. "Okay. We'll say they went into a rehab program." Xantha laughed, "Yeah, they went into The Program. That works . . ."

3

If men were angels, no government would be necessary.

—James Madison

All men would be tyrants if they could.

—Abigail Adams

Within the confines of humanity lie two very distinctive traits. The first is the inherent desire for survival. The second is to destroy anyone or anything that stands in the way of that desire. Throughout history, this attribute has been proven to be true.

Roger Bajor always seemed to desire a leadership post. Be it when he was eight years old playing shortstop on the ten-and-over Little League team or when he was the third chair in the wind ensemble in high school or when he was the first sophomore at the University of Virginia to be voted into the student council in seventy-five years, leadership seemed to gravitate to him his entire life. Sometimes people reach out for leadership, and sometimes leadership reaches out for them.

Devouring books and knowledge, Roger had an unfair advantage right from the beginning of his life. An only child, Roger's parents were both leaders in their own right. His mother Barbara was an eighth-grade teacher, while his father James was a writer. His mother was voted "Teacher of the Year" so often that after the fourth time, she withdrew her name for future consideration. His father was a top-selling author in the beginning of his career, and he had done so well at that time that he had occasionally been compensated for just an *idea* that he had brought to his agent and publishing company. They paid James just to have the rights to his mind.

To top it off, Roger's grandmother on his father's side had been a librarian for most of her life. Every year, for his birthday, starting at the age of ten, Roger received a complete collection of last year's encyclopedia, since the library would simply throw them out when they received their current year's supply. Roger would come home from school and pick a letter of the alphabet and just start reading. In time, of course, the encyclopedia became valuable not only for his personal use, but as a resource to be used in his scholastic career. His grades all throughout his career had been nothing but stellar. Indeed, he did not achieve "straight As," but that seemed to work in his favor. Roger knew what it felt like to aim for perfection, but then come up short. But instead of curling into a ball and ceasing to function, Roger used his "failures" as motivation to simply be better.

Even in sports, whenever he failed, his father would quote one of heroes and say to Roger, "You lost today, kid, but that doesn't mean you have to like it."

Roger was the consummate "well-rounded" individual. He knew how to play almost any card game, but he also was excellent at sewing and repairing garments. He knew how to cook and even mixed drinks for his mother and father's many dinner guests, and he was doing it by the age of twelve. He was acutely athletic, but he devoted his time to only baseball by the age of thirteen. He could have participated in almost any sport at the time, and he would have been successful, but his attention to detail, plus the intellectual strength necessary to play baseball naturally drew him to that game above all others.

Roger had always been able to explain away why he didn't like something, especially certain sports. Football, he had always claimed, was a game so focused on the physical nature of its participants, that it could be simplified down to the phrase, "just beat the guy in front of you." Right or wrong, that's just how he felt, and it just wasn't challenging enough for him. Basketball had the similar trait of physicality, but it also had the base emotion of intimidation and chest-beating of which he simply was not a proponent. Indeed, Roger had said later in his life that had he devoted his time to playing basketball instead of baseball, he probably would have gotten himself into a brawl or two. In his mind, he was saving people from that because he wasn't going to lose those brawls, and it probably would have been vicious if it had come to that.

But while baseball became the sport to which he had, henceforth, devoted all of his time, there was something else that Roger embraced almost at the same time: martial arts.

He had heard several of his baseball teammates talking about their forms and competitions and had begun to ask them about how to become a member of their group. Interestingly enough, the players who were taking martial arts were more than happy to explain what was necessary to succeed at Tae Kwon Do (which was the martial art they all took). Roger immediately gravitated to the comradery that Tae Kwon Do embraced, and how being a part of their martial art school brought them closer together as teammates in every way.

A natural athlete, Roger mastered the basics fairly quickly and, after a few months of attending class four times a week, had achieved his green belt. Once someone gets their green belt, they begin to spar with each other. All the punches and kicks they had learned as a white and yellow belt were now to be put to the test. His instructor, Mr. Paul (his first name was Frank, but no one *ever* called him that), had told Roger that the school usually loses about 50 percent of the graduating class when they become green belts. Some people just didn't like to get hit.

During their very first sparring match, Mr. Paul made it a point to be the first person that the newly crowned green belts fight. This way, Mr. Paul can explain what the expectation is for his students from this day forward. They would put on their gear, which included head, foot, and hand protection, along with a mouth guard. He would encourage his new green belts to hit him, and then would help them with target area and strength of punch. Usually, it was the strength of punch that needed to be adjusted first.

Some students simply punched too hard, while others just tip-tapped, as he would say.

"Fifty percent . . . that's how hard you should punch or

kick," Mr. Paul would always instruct. "That allows you to hit someone at a rate of power where the one being punched can feel it, and the one throwing it feels like they are doing something."

But there was something else in play, something that Mr. Paul would not initially talk about.

Control. His students *must* have control. They must eventually throw a punch or kick *knowing* where it was going to land and at what rate of power. Mr. Paul knew that he could talk and instruct all day long, but the experience of hitting (and being hit) was priceless. Inevitably, with his new green belts, he would allow a certain level of wildness and then correct that wildness with a punch or kick that would allow his student to know that this was for real from now on.

There were so many elements of martial arts that went into being a good practitioner that only practice and participation—and trial and error—would suffice. Mr. Paul, of course, knew this. Defense was just as important, if not more important than, offense. Indeed, offense was borne out of defense as far as Mr. Paul was concerned, but the only way to make that clear was to cause pain, albeit a mild amount of it. Mr. Paul would snap out a strong punch or kick to the body to let his student know that they were unacceptably vulnerable. Only when a student had made the decision to protect themselves while being offensive would they inevitably begin to learn control.

Roger's first sparring session was predictably one-sided, of course. But Mr. Paul realized right away that Roger had no intention of being overly zealous with his attacks. In fact, Roger would never punch or kick until *after* Mr. Paul did. It was classic "punch, counterpunch" for a while, until Mr. Paul broke off a combination of punches and kicks that placed Roger on the mat. Undeterred, Roger rose from the mattress and assumed the opening sparring position. Mr. Paul was impressed, and he put that in the bank.

Martial arts, while allowing Roger to stay in shape year-round, also helped him both with his agility in baseball, as well as his mental acuity in all other areas of his life. Taking up martial arts and baseball at the same time, by the time he entered high school, Roger felt that he was becoming a well-oiled machine in every facet of his life. The beginning of his high school career was, truly, the beginning of the building of Roger.

His grades were exceptional, his friendships plentiful, and his athletic career forever promising, Roger seemed destined for greatness . . . and he was.

Many stories were borne out of Roger's existence, but one in particular revolved around a martial arts competition that he, incredibly and remarkably, had to be convinced to attend. Roger was never one to place any real value on martial arts competition, since they were not, in his opinion, a real indicator of true skill. Indeed, these competitions seemed to be catered in a way that anyone could win, no matter what their skill level. This irked Roger no end, for he worked extremely hard on his craft, as did all of his friends. And then they would walk into one of these "competitions" where there would be all of these special rules, (such as no punches to the head, for example), and he felt it was like fighting with one hand behind his back.

It was patently unfair . . . and he loathed that. He always maintained that it took courage to voice the opinion that something was unfair, but he had very few allies in this area.

These competitions were meant to level the playing field to allow all levels of skill to compete on an equal setting, which simply did not interest Roger in any way.

In any case, here Roger was, competing using their rules, which stifled *his* rules. And he was winning. And advancing. And the next thing you knew, Roger was competing in the finals of his very first tournament. And against the defending champion, who happened to be the master of a rival academy. After all this, Roger stood in the center ring being cheered on by his friends and his school, and he loved it.

"Life builds to moments," Roger would always say, "and you either grab them, or they pass you by."

The match began slowly, with each person desperate to feel out their opponent. Roger's opponent scored first, with a lightning-fast kick to the head.

"Point!" the referee shouted, as they returned to their mark.

Roger rushed in, scoring on a straight kick that was partially blocked, but it got through anyway. It was one to one. The winner would be the first to three.

Roger could see that the scoring of a point had upset his opponent, and Roger intended to use that to his advantage.

"Anger and rage affects your judgment," he remembered being told long ago, and here it was being borne out right in front of him.

Within nearly every discipline lies a turning point that no one can deny. It is the first and most memorable step toward the mastering of that specialty. It could takes days, months, or years to reveal itself, but it is there nonetheless. Many athletes refer to it as "when the game slows down for you." Almost every great athlete—and some not-so-great ones—knows precisely what is being referred to here.

The sensation revolves around the momentary domination of the moment at hand. Whether it be the snap of a football, a play at the plate, or a shot with no time left on the clock, no one would argue that the moment exists.

And it reveals itself so benignly that, sometimes, the moment is only realized after the moment has passed. Oddly, there is tragedy here. For while the moment exists, the performer has difficulty enjoying it, if you will. That is to say, while a batter is at the plate with a full count in the bottom of the ninth with players on second and third, that batter—if he or she is either a great athlete or at least at the top of their game at that moment—will only be focusing on the job at hand. Indeed, should that batter be successful and strike a clean single into right field, scoring both the tying and the winning run, those who are witnessing it will have to tell the one executing it that this moment was, in fact, great.

Many times, when a hero is asked about their heroic moment, they profess to have no memory of it or that they were lost in the moment so much that they have no recollection of it. It is, in fact, an impressive trait that one could easily mark down to what it is to be a human being. Indeed, this trait of being lost in the moment is a part of something much bigger: the human condition.

So it certainly stands to reason that this trait, while being a disappointment for the one who accomplishes the feat in that they barely remember it, is an absolute joy for the ones who witness it. In fact, many heroes rely heavily on eyewitness testimony as to whether the event for which they are being celebrated for actually happened.

+

Roger was tied with an opponent whom no one would argue was more talented and more accomplished than he was. But that just meant that his opponent had a lot more to lose, and that can certainly be a tremendous disadvantage. If Roger's opponent won, then that was simply what was supposed to happen. But, if Roger was successful, then it would be an incredible upset. And since Roger had nothing to lose . . . he could afford to gamble; he could afford to take risks.

Roger squared off with his opponent with the score tied at one. Oddly enough, Roger could sense a level of overconfidence oozing from across the mat. Before it even happened, Roger saw his opponent jump toward him, slightly out of control, trying to strike him with a front kick. As if in slow motion, Roger stepped aside, allowed his opponent to pass, and dug in. Roger snapped out a left uppercut to the midsection and scored a rousing point that staggered his man.

"Point!" the ref shouted, and there was a loud gasp throughout the room as everyone's attention now turned to this match.

Roger was one point away from victory. A sudden rush of adrenaline flowed through Roger's body. He tried not to get lost in the moment, but, having never been there before, he was a hostage to his raw emotions.

Roger no longer saw his opponent as a person or even as an opponent anymore. To Roger, he was a faceless enemy, nothing more, nothing less. Up two to one, Roger tried not to squander his good fortune. They reset and charged at each other, ending up nearly back to back. Roger hesitated, for he had never been in this position physically before, and he didn't know what to do. Then he felt a smack to the back of his own head with a hook kick. Roger had forgotten that the back of the head was a target area, goddamn it!

"Point!" the official shouted.

Roger had given away his advantage almost as quickly as he had attained it. Hooray. They both reset, and then, the game slowed down for him.

Roger couldn't win straight up . . . he knew it. He also knew that deception was just a totally bitch way to victory. The old saying goes, if your opponent resorts to a trick play, like the Statue of Liberty play, or the hidden ball trick, then, if you survive it, you'd win going away. But—and this a huge *but*—if you pick your spot, throw in a trick play at that moment in time where you either win or lose in a flash, you might just gain the admiration of all involved.

Roger moved in, as the world slowed down for him, he leaped at his faceless enemy. Maintaining his balance, and being in complete control, Roger threw a high block, incidentally covering the eyes of his opponent. Banking on the fact that when someone appears to attack the head and eyes, they instinctively raise their hands to protect themselves, Roger struck. His opponent's hands went up, if only for a split second, and Roger snapped out a straight punch to the midsection, ending the bout.

"Point! Winner!" the referee shouted, and it was as if a dam that held people back had broken, releasing them onto the mat. Within the cacophony of hoots, hollers, yips, and shouts lay a champion. The most unlikely champion, but a champion nonetheless. And his name was Roger Bajor.

+

That bout was a snapshot of the mental toughness of Roger Bajor. And, as his life progressed, a most telling attribute began to reveal itself. This trait was a little distressing because it foretold an absolute truth about one Roger Bajor: he was at his best when he was emotionally ice cold. Just like almost any warrior, it was a truth that both elevated him and dogged him his entire life.

Roger had always lamented, as he moved through his life, that he was most successful when he detached from his emotions. Indeed, it was proved many times over that Roger was a killer who was most deadly when he simply refused to lose. When victory simply *had* to be the outcome, Roger sacrificed a great deal to get to that place. There is a great debt to pay for this attribute, and Roger had always been prepared to pay it.

But that *also* came at a price. Roger's circle of friends grew smaller, and his footprint on the world shrank as well. And while Roger's accomplishments were many, those who *really* knew him were few and far between.

And as the game slowed down for him, that mastery tended to isolate him as well. People react very differently to isolation. Some embrace it as a welcome respite to the world that is more cruel than good, while others see it for what it is: a necessary tool of greatness. Roger had essentially been able to construct a mental algorithm for both coping with problems at precisely the moment they reveal themselves and creating the solutions necessary to solve those problems. It is this level of problem solving that initially drew him to Xantha Grasso. She thought as he did, and she was able to find a solution to a problem that, unbeknownst to Xantha, Roger had been working on for over thirty years—and at great personal and professional cost. Xantha, without knowing it, was the last part of Roger's algorithmic approach, and he was the first part of Xantha's.

4

That is what Xantha Grasso's friend Saul Vitetto saw, and this is why Saul became Xantha's executive officer in every sense of the word. Holding that unofficial title, Saul embraced precisely what Xantha embraced, virtually from the beginning and virtually all the time.

Without even knowing it, Saul had dreamed of his position in The Program, or at least Xantha's place within it, all of his life. Dreams had become terribly important to him at an extremely early age. Saul had studied psychologists and read their books since he had begun to decipher what his dreams meant to him. He had a particularly terrifying dream when he was eleven years old, and that dream held him hostage for over a month. Saul had begun to fear sleep, lest he dream his horrible dream again.

His parents had arranged for Saul to see a therapist, and this had set in motion a lifetime of therapy for Saul. In all fairness to him, Saul desperately required that which therapy had to offer: a neutral party to bounce his thoughts and overactive mind off of.

Having become a product of therapy, Saul, in turn, was beginning to acquire a particular talent that would continue to serve him for the rest of his life. A natural empath, Saul could read the room, or even a person, almost instantaneously.

A lean man with good taste, Saul Vitetto grew up in Brooklyn, but he did the trek through "guinea gulch" from Brooklyn to Jersey City, with a little time spent in Patterson, and then from Elizabeth to northwest New Jersey, settling in Hunterdon County by the time he was about to start high school. Believe it or not, there are a lot of Italians in northwest New Jersey.

Saul's parents slowly divorced as they passed each other on the downside of their marriage over the course of about four years. Typically brave and mostly practical, Johnny and Marie knew very soon in their marriage that it wasn't going to last. That didn't seem to stop them from having a big family (five kids counting Saul), or having family dinners at their house every Sunday as long as Saul could remember. Those Sundays were a raucous affair, with many relatives making the trip from Brooklyn.

So Saul became a child of divorce, which does not make him special, but that clearly motivated him for the rest of his life.

"Children of divorce never trust again," was a phrase that Saul remembered hearing quite often as he moved from childhood into early adulthood. But Saul always added that all he wanted was to trust a small group of people, and to have them trust him too.

Saul also had an incredible, awesome trait: he could tell anyone what to do softly and politely, but in a way that left little room for discussion. Saul was also a high-end tech guy, who had high-end tech friends. He was like that gamer friend who could build the system on which the games were played and then build into that system a self-destruct sequence. A smart man.

Saul's meeting of Agent Grasso was by complete coincidence, of course. At least, that is the story Xantha told. Xantha was in her third year at UVA (having gained the endorsement and written recommendation of Roger Bajor), and she saw Saul, a first-year student, from across the quad. Xantha had begun to hone her observational skills, and was quietly folding them into her analytical skills, thereby creating quite the weapon of herself, if she didn't mind saying so herself.

She watched from afar as she saw Saul, alone, intervene into a potentially difficult and dangerous situation where three boys were beginning to argue about something. It appeared to be every man for himself, and Xantha, intrigued, moved herself within listening distance and watched the circumstances unfold.

"Where's my money?" yelled the first boy, a shorter blond kid who was well-dressed, yet appeared disheveled.

"I told you, you'll get it on Friday," the taller, scrawny boy yelled back. "My parents will send it, and I'll get it to you. Chill, bro."

"Don't tell me to chill, man," the first boy shot back.

The third boy, a short, stocky man, started to circle behind Blondie without being seen.

"Just make sure you get it to me by Friday, or you'll be paying points."

"Points?" the tall one questioned. "What the hell are 'points'?"

The third boy moved even further behind and out of

sight of Blondie. Saul moved too, and none of the three saw it. Xantha did, and she eased closer.

"Interest, you idiot. You pay interest on the principal of what you owe. I don't wait for my money without penalty forever, you know."

Tall Boy moved closer to Blondie, while Shorty kept moving behind Blondie. Xantha deduced that Tall Boy and Shorty were friends. Saul seemed to see that too.

Blondie talked in a calm voice.

"Points just motivates someone to pay me faster is all, just relax. You said Friday. Let's just say Friday." Tall Boy said, "Or else I pay interest?"

"Yeah. Interest."

"We'll see," said Tall Boy. And then Shorty made his move. And so did Saul.

As Shorty raised his arm to strike Blondie on the head, Saul swooped in and just flat-out tackled Shorty. It was filthy. Saul decked him like he was sacking the quarterback in the championship game. Blondie turned around, fists at the ready, and saw that Saul had it under control. Saul was laying on top of the stunned and sacked Shorty, and he looked up at Blondie with a nod.

Blondie turned back to Tall Boy, fists raised, and said "Friday, or you deal with him, not me."

Tall Boy backed down, turned, and walked away. Saul let Shorty up, and then watched as he walked away in the other direction.

Blondie walked up to Saul. "Thanks, I guess. What's your name?"

"Saul. Saul Vitetto." Blondie shook his hand. "My name is Thomas. Thomas Duphrane. Just call me Tommy."

Saul smiled, "Okay, Tommy. See you around campus."

Xantha smiled too and walked away, making a note to herself that she needed to get to know those two a little better.

Saul and Tommy parted, but they would clearly meet again. As friends, to be sure. But little did they know just how close they were to become.

+

It started out like any other day—as most days do—but the day was to become one of the most important days in the history of The Program and a watershed moment for both Saul and Tommy.

Over the last couple of weeks, Saul and Tommy had become quite friendly. While they had virtually the same cluster of classes, they only had one that was at the same time: Modern British Lit. And they both agreed, as they sat side by side in the back of the room, that this class was the most boring class that they had ever taken. A required course to graduate (students had to take a 200-level English course to obtain their diploma in Liberal Arts), both Saul and Tommy felt they were being forced to take a course they cared nothing about.

Indeed, they both came to the same conclusion that Modern British Lit was a course that had zero British authors. Oscar Wilde, James Joyce, playwright Samuel Beckett, and Joseph Conrad (of Polish–British decent) were the authors they were studying. Only Beckett tickled their fancy with his *Waiting for Godot* masterpiece. The rest just seemed both maudlin and morose as they plodded through their Irish upbringing.

In any case, it was their American History classes that

stimulated both of them in a way that they would meet together for about an hour on a bench on the edge of campus and bandy about what they had learned that day.

On this particular day, Saul and Tommy were conversing about the causes and effects of World War II, and how they were relevant even today. Saul had begun to understand the parameters in which fascism had flourished, while Tommy actually began to understand the lure of communism both before and after World War II.

Tommy began, "You know, when you look around at the world today and see how ridiculous it is for the everyday worker, I understand their frustration."

Saul smirked as Tommy continued. "What? You don't understand their plight? I mean, if every worker in the US realized the power that they would have if they all united under one cause, and just didn't show up for work one day, that the corporate establishment would have no choice but to deal with and bargain with them."

Saul smiled and spoke. "I can hire one half of the working class to kill the other half."

Tommy smiled as well. "Jay Gould," Tommy said. "You know, actually, the struggle to unite the working class, to fight against all forms of racist and other prejudices, is an attempt to *prevent* Gould's boast from being carried forward in policy—which capitalists in their use of some workers, immigrants, and minorities to break strikes, along with police and militia drawn from the working class, have done many times in the past, especially before the enactment of federal labor laws in the 1930s."

Saul looked astonished. "That was a long way home, brother. How did you even remember all of that?"

Tommy smiled. "We were studying the Gilded Age earlier today. You know, that age from 1880 through the 1930s. Industrial Revolution, child labor, and the rise of unions." Tommy tapped his head. "It's still fresh in my mind. 'Workers of the world *unite!*'"

They both chuckled, and then Saul began again.

"Do you see that homeless person on the bench over there?"

"Yeah, I've been watching that guy the whole time we've been sitting here," said Tommy.

"Well, we have no idea what his story is, but there he lies. Motionless, probably broke, and not a care in the world." At that moment, someone walked by the man and casually dropped a piece of trash directly onto him as he was lying on the bench. The man did not even flinch. "You see? That guy is no longer encumbered with the attitudes and expectations of this society. Someone just threw trash on him, and he didn't even move."

Tommy questioned, "So? Maybe he's asleep. Maybe he's exhausted. Or maybe he's an addict or a drunk."

Saul finished, "Or maybe he's the happiest he's ever been in his entire life." Tommy sat a moment and considered this last point and smirked. "Maybe. But I doubt it."

Saul continued. "The point is, that guy appears to have essentially 'given up on life.' He took his shot and, for reasons perhaps both known and unknown, he has acquiesced authority over his existence."

Tommy was listening as Saul made his point.

"That guy is forfeiting control over most of his life. Whether it be financially, economically, socially, or even legally, that guy is allowing all those around him, from now on, to make those decisions. It's over, he knows it, and the responsibility for him now falls to others, most likely the government."

Tommy shrugged in mild agreement.

Saul finished his thought. "Do you know what that is? It's a form of fascism where the individual is allowing those who are perceived to be 'strong' to rule over those who are equally perceived to be 'weak.'"

"People scream and yell about fascism and how horrible and awful it is, yet there it sits. On that bench. A citizen *inviting* the government to take over his life." Tommy nodded and edited his previous phrase. "Maybe, but we really do not know any of that yet."

Just then, a motorcycle absolutely *roared* by the man on the bench. Nothing. Saul and Tommy sat up in their bench and peered at the man.

"Did you see *that*? That guy didn't move at all!"

They both looked at each other with concern and stood up.

"Maybe . . . maybe we should go over there and make sure he's okay."

Tommy nodded in agreement, and they both cautiously approached the sleeping man. As they got closer, they could see that the man's eyes were half closed and clouded over. Saul and Tommy quickened their pace, and soon they were upon him.

"Ooh! This guy *stinks*!" said Saul.

Tommy agreed. Saul found a stick and poked at the man. Nothing. He appeared to have soiled his pants, but that wasn't what they were smelling. They looked at each other with a knowing look, and then Saul pulled out his cell phone to dial 911.

"Nine-one-one. What's your emergency?"

"Yeah hello, this is Saul Vitetto over at the University of Virginia. I just walked up to a bench where this homeless guy is sleeping. He's not moving, and his eyes are kind of cloudy and glossed over."

"Has he blinked at all?" asked the operator.

Saul remarked matter-of-factly, "Actually, he hasn't."

The operator spoke again. "Have you touched him at all?"

"No . . . I just poked him with a stick. He didn't react at all." Saul said.

"Where are you?" said the operator. "I'm going to send a unit. Actually, is this your phone?"

Saul said, "Yes."

"Okay, I'll just send the police to your GPS on your phone." The operator was silent for a moment. "Okay, I have it. Can you wait there for the cops? They'll be there in ten minutes."

Saul said, "Sure, we'll wait," and he hung up his phone. "The cops are coming. She said to wait for them."

"Okay."

Saul put his hands in his pockets and shrugged as Tommy looked equally perplexed. Ten minutes later, the police arrived, along with an ambulance. In a dizzying array of police procedure, the cops simply moved Saul and Tommy to the curb, while the EMT took a few vitals, loaded the man onto a gurney, stuffed him inside the ambulance, and drove off. One cop asked one question.

"Who is Saul Vitetto?"

Saul raised his hand.

"Sign here please."

The cop put out his phone, and Saul signed with his

finger. Without another word, the cop climbed back into his car and drove away, leaving Saul and Tommy standing next to an empty bench that once held the body of an unknown man.

Tommy just looked at Saul.

"I guess I gotta go to class. I'll meet you later at the pub."

"Yeah . . . okay. See ya."

5

Tommy Duphrane was born the son of a preacher whose wife, Tommy's mother, tragically died upon his birth. The cruelest of ironies (the gift of life at the cost of one) was not lost upon Tommy's father, Jeff. A man of God at the time, Jeff's faith was immediately staggered forever. His mother's death changed his father, Pastor Jeff, and not necessarily for the better. A pious man and a religious man, Tommy's father took a darker, angrier path after he was born, and Tommy knew nothing of how the man lived before his birth. Tommy only relied on the stories and memories of others as he moved through life an unintentional only child. Pastor Jeff never found love again, and one could easily argue that it was mostly because he was no longer looking.

While growing up in the simplest of households across the street from his father's Methodist church, Tommy would hear his father praying loudly somewhere inside the house, yelling at God. More than once, Tommy heard his father sobbing, begging God to take him from this place.

"Have mercy upon me Lord!" Tommy would hear his father shout late at night. "I can't stand the pain any longer! Release me from this rage and desolation!"

But there would always be a pause, and then an affirmation of faith.

"Forgive me Lord, for I am weak, and full of fear. You're right, of course. I shall suffer for Thomas. He is a good boy."

And then Pastor Jeff would get himself together, rise to his feet, wipe his eyes, and get on with his life.

Many who watched from afar could not understand how Pastor Jeff could do it. Most presupposed that Tommy gave him reason to live, and, as Tommy grew older, anyone could see that Pastor Jeff, a broken man, adored his only son. Never overprotective, Pastor Jeff was still quite cautious when it came to his son. After the age of five, when Tommy began kindergarten, Pastor Jeff was able to return his own life to a sense of normalcy in the only way he knew how: he simply *threw* himself into his church and the Word of God.

While taking a bit of a sabbatical when Tommy was born, Pastor Jeff was surviving by simply going through the motions, both in life and as a member and the pastor of his church. Most would have given Pastor Jeff a pass if he had simply begun to just "mail in" his pastoral duties, but Pastor Jeff genuinely impressed both with his sermons and with how he was dealing with his flock. But that was the limit of his existence at that point. In truth, had Pastor Jeff not had his church duties to occupy his time during this extremely trying time, who knows where he would have ended up? Tommy slowly began to realize what had happened the day he was born, and he slowly began to gravitate to the church as a whole in his youth.

As Tommy moved through elementary school and then into middle school, he began to spend more time in the sanctuary listening to his father's sermons, rather than staying downstairs in the youth rooms taking Sunday school classes with the rest of the children. His father's words began to hypnotize and inspire him, and by the age of thirteen, Tommy had become a regular within the adult church community.

Within the Methodist community, the pastor would sometimes be forced to be reassigned to another church every three or four years. But at the time of Tommy's birth, the Methodist church had begun to move away from this practice. That was fortunate for Tommy and his father, for they needed the support of the church now more than ever. And it also allowed Pastor Jeff's flock to grow stronger in their faith, while also allowing Tommy a degree of stability within his fragile existence. Indeed, by the time Tommy had reached the age of fourteen, the bishop and the district superintendent had both agreed that Pastor Jeff could remain with his church at least until Tommy had graduated high school.

Perhaps this level of "job security" in place motivated what happened next. Pastor Jeff, on the fifteenth anniversary of both his son's birth and his wife's death, was preparing a sermon for the ages. Indeed, he felt called to do this because of the fact that this day was falling on a Sunday as well. All the stars seemed to align for this moment, and Pastor Jeff was not going to let it pass him by. Pastor Jeff was going to grab it.

+

There's nothing like discussing "The Meaning of Life" over a few drinks, and that was precisely what Saul and Tommy began to do just a few hours after their encounter with the man on the bench. It was Friday night, so both Saul and Tommy had no classes the next day and planned to drink as long as they wished. Sitting at a two-top table in the corner of Trinity Irish Pub, both men sought to isolate themselves for this particular talk. They weren't rattled by their experience, but both clearly had some thoughts about it.

Ordering four shots of vodka (two apiece) and a cheese pizza, Saul and Tommy toasted themselves with the first shot, and then gave each other knowing glances for the second shot.

"To the unknown Man on the Bench," said Saul.

Tommy clinked his glass and threw it down. Their pizza arrived, and they both took a slice, and then they both became eager to discuss their day.

"That was . . . weird, I guess," said Tommy. "I don't know. It just seemed so final and rushed."

"Yeah, like they couldn't get that guy out of there fast enough."

"I wonder who he was," Saul asked out loud. There was a quiet pause as both men posited what to say next. Finally, Tommy spoke.

"Do you want to go find out?"

"Find out what?"

"Who this guy was and where he is."

"Sure. Okay."

They both gulped down their remaining pizza, paid the bill, and stood outside the bar wondering what to do next.

"Well, I saw it was just local cops, and the station is

right over there," Saul said. "I mean, we could always just ask, right?"

Tommy thought about it, shrugged, and then agreed. "Yeah. Okay. Let's go."

They both walked the couple of blocks and found themselves in front of the police station in a few minutes. Without speaking, they walked in and approached the front desk. A slightly overweight gentleman in uniform was filling out paperwork, and Tommy got his attention.

"Um. Good evening, officer."

The policeman looked up and nodded.

"I know this might sound weird, but my friend and I called in a . . . well, I don't know . . . there was a man on a bench on campus. We both go to UVA over there. Anyway, we called in this guy, and an ambulance came and whisked him away."

The cop at the desk seemed unimpressed.

Tommy continued. "Can I ask what happened to him? Like, where he is?"

The policeman looked down, and then he rustled some papers.

"Pretty slow today, I bet I have his paperwork right here."

He fiddled some more, reached over to some folders, and then found it.

"Here it is. 'Unknown DOA found on park bench. No name, no ID. Sent to the coroner, designated HJD.'"

Saul asked, "What does 'HJD' mean?"

The officer answered matter-of-factly, "Homeless John Doe."

Saul and Tommy looked at each other, then back to the desk cop. "Well, then what?"

The cop laid it out for them. When a DOA is found with no ID and is apparently homeless, the coroner declares the cause of death, usually without an actual autopsy, and then waits fourteen days for someone to come in and file a missing person report. If no report is filed, the morgue decides what to do next. Usually, they take a bunch of photos, get some samples, file it away, and cremate the body for health purposes. Most of these cases end up with dead ends all around. No one claims the body, no one files a missing person report, and the cremated body sits in an urn in a room for 365 days before being filed into a warehouse up state somewhere.

Tommy and Saul stood in stony silence as they listened to this disc jockey calmly lay out how someone just essentially disappears from the face of the Earth without so much as the quietest of whimpers. They both thanked the officer for his time and then walked out, stunned.

Standing in front of the station, both of them, hands in their pockets, seemed resigned to the dead man's fate.

"Well, that sucks," Tommy said. "We don't even know his name. That guy lived a life, and then he's gone. And I doubt that even one person cares at all."

"Yeah," said Saul, his mind racing a bit. "They just made a guy . . . disappear."

6

Pastor Jeff was about to deliver a sermon that he felt as though he had been working on for nearly a year. Indeed, he was taking bits and pieces of this sermon from all parts of his life, so this one was going to be comprehensive in nature. But all Tommy knew was that he was graduating high school that week, and he was going to the University of Virginia in the fall. Tommy was eighteen years old, and his life was just beginning.

Pastor Jeff had been working long and hard on this particular sermon, and he would privately admit to himself that he was quite proud of the points he was making within it. These were sermons that achieved the rarified air of being chocked full of "words to live by" as far as he was concerned, and Pastor Jeff hoped and prayed that those who heard it today would somehow remember it forever.

As he approached the pulpit, Pastor Jeff looked out among his flock and was pleased to see that the sanctuary was indeed filled to near capacity. He sat, listened to the opening prayer, heard the first two hymns, and then stood to begin his message, which he entitled, "Why Are We Here?" He opened with a prayer of his own, ending it with what he had always said.

"It is my hope, it is my prayer, it is my expectation, that God would meet us in this place." And then he began. "Why are we here?" he asked.

He always liked to open with a nearly impossible question so as to garner the most attention that he could. A small amount of laughter and chuckling wafted over his flock.

"Indeed, along with the Golden Rule, this question has dominated humanity since the dawn of time. But I would like to *answer* that question today, if you don't mind, so pay attention."

The quiet tittering turned into open guffawing. A great start.

"Indeed, why are we here? One could easily argue that all of you have gone through your lives, gone to school, graduated like my son, who is here today, then gone to work, made some money, started a family, woke up today, put on your Sunday best, and came to church today to hear me preach. That is why you are here."

Open laughter, followed by applause, happened next, and, always the performer, Pastor Jeff smiled, waited until his audience died down, and then said, "You're darn right!"

He continued. "But, of course, this is not what I am talking about. No friends, I am talking more about 'Why are we here as God's children,' and maybe I'm asking the question 'What makes us so special?' It has long been speculated that the power to reason is what puts us above the everyday animal, and this"—Pastor Jeff held up the Bible—"is the evidence of that achievement."

Light applause filled the room.

"But I am not talking about God and Jesus, per se. Not yet, anyway. No, I speak about the ability to put words to ideas to truth and fact. In short, I speak about what *language* has done to allow humans to rise up.

"Language is what sets us apart, dear brothers and sisters. Language is how we communicate. Language is a tool that we use. Indeed, one can argue that language is the *only* tool that we have at our disposal. Whether it be with words, actions, signs, or some other way, it is language that makes us who we are both as a race and as a people, God-fearing or not, religious or not, evil or not."

Pastor Jeff took a sip of water, then went on to quote philosophers and laypeople alike as he moved effortlessly through the derivation of thought and word, and how these words bring us either closer or further away from God. He continued an impressive argument that moved from language (the spoken word) into how he genuinely felt that God spoke to all of them: through what he called "the art of knowing." He used one of his favorite quotes, saying that it was John F. Kennedy who said it best when he remarked that, "There is something immoral about not following your instincts." Pastor Jeff used that example as a way to illustrate how we all "know" what to do but fight with ourselves constantly as to how to achieve this.

His sermon went from language to "knowing" to this finite existence within the mortal coil. The phrase *mortal coil* Pastor Jeff explained, is a poetic term for the troubles of daily life and the strife and suffering of the world. It is used in the sense of a burden to be carried or abandoned. To "shuffle off this *mortal coil*" is to die, he explained, and is exemplified in the "To be, or not to be" soliloquy in Shakespeare's *Hamlet*.

He went on to explain that Shakespeare was the brilliant interpreter of biblical elements into a way that the rest of us can understand. William Shakespeare, Pastor Jeff continued to expound, was the genius that the world needed to enlighten us all into the understanding of the most basic tenets of existence: heaven and hell, good and evil, and right versus wrong. And Pastor Jeff concluded his sermon with the fire and brimstone that comes with the understanding that while we are all mortal, there are worse things than death.

"Indeed," Pastor Jeff concluded, "knowing that we are mortal is an extremely powerful tool toward becoming the best person you can be, and the greatest servant of God possible."

He went on to tie it all together, saying language is our stepping out of the chaos and into the order of the world. The Bible gave all of us both a roadmap and a reason for being, while coupling them together gives humans both life and *a life*. And this gives life *meaning*. Pastor Jeff was clear about how this might be all that God has guaranteed for us.

"And while how you live can either save or destroy both Life and your life, listening to the 'art of knowing' can, and will, save your *soul*."

The attention of his congregation was at the highest it has ever been at this moment, and Pastor Jeff ended his sermon with this, from Walt Whitman:

Oh me! Oh life! of the questions of these recurring,
Of the endless trains of the faithless, of cities fill'd with the foolish,
Of myself forever reproaching myself, (for who more foolish than I, and who more faithless?)
Of eyes that vainly crave the light, of the objects mean, of the struggle ever renew'd,
Of the poor results of all, of the plodding and sordid crowds I see around me,
Of the empty and useless years of the rest, with the rest me intertwined,
The question, O me! so sad, recurring—What good amid these, O me, O life?
Answer.
That you are here—that life exists and identity,
That the powerful play goes on, and you may contribute a verse . . ."

And then, for effect, Pastor Jeff leaned in and said the last line again.

"'That the *powerful play* goes *on*, and *you* may contribute a verse.'" He concluded, "What will *your* verse *be*?" And then closed his eyes and said, "Will you pray with me?"

After a silence that may have lasted thirty seconds, Pastor Jeff simply said, "Come . . . Holy Spirit."

And he stepped down and seated himself quietly. After a pause, someone began to clap, then another, and another, until everyone was clapping, then standing, and then roaring in approval. It was a moment for the ages and one that Tommy would never forget . . .

Ever.

It is an impressive feat, this thing called life, and it is not to be entered into lightly. Indeed, it is the ease in which life can be created that can give almost anyone pause, for how can something so important, so remarkable, and so potentially devastating, be so categorically simple? And life as it is known is not the same as a life well-lived.

There are thousands of parameters in which to judge the quality of life. Those parameters seem to revolve around faith, health, relationships, and a myriad of other elements that surround all of these things. For some reason, the question of productivity, efficiency, and competence rank high upon that peripheral list.

How can one judge whether a life is well-lived? Or a failure? Or a success? How is this to be mitigated? Indeed, there is a sound argument about God and salvation that revolves around the sentiment that if God knows everything about me, and that we are all made in God's image, then how can one be judged, when the time comes, as someone who is *not* saved? Comically, one could say that "this is all God's fault" if He is truly in control of everyone and everything. This is not a popular sentiment, of course, but it is still considered the lightest of criticisms that holds the lightest of value.

In any case, were anyone to invoke logic, then logic clearly dictates that it is essentially the "free will" of the human spirit that demands responsibility for one's actions. Some people simply have no choice, while others are woefully at a disadvantage, and still others simply have no tools at all to cope with this thing called life.

So what is one to do with this information? Why does any of this matter? And what can be done to master the chaos? Well, if it were up to Tommy, he would always defer, time and again, to his father's words, which stipulated that we are what we do, both within and without. One thing that Pastor Jeff would say, time and time again, is that people always ask, "Why me?" and to this, he would always answer, "Why not me?" What makes one so special that they would surmise that they do not deserve anything bad to happen to them? It's exactly that which makes them so special, Tommy would answer, and this is what serves to define us both as a person and as a human being.

"None of us were promised a pain-free life," Tommy would always say to himself when confronted with the trials and tribulations of this thing called life. And yet, Tommy always understood that God only tests those who can take it. And it is this mentality that stood to shape Tommy as a man, both now and forever. And he carried that like a badge for all of his life.

And as he continued to move through his life, and through his education, both scholastically and spiritually, Tommy would always hold onto the promise that his better angels would eventually guide his every move. But, not just yet. He finished his drink alone at the bar, then got up to leave. He was meeting Saul later, even though it was past 10:00 p.m. It was important.

They were both going to meet Xantha. She had something to ask them. Tommy believed that she was going to ask him to be the best version of himself. They would find out together.

Saul and Tommy were given instructions to arrive in the conference room at 10:00 p.m. Bring only your ID, she said, and she let it be known that they were both going to be interviewed together.

The room was actually one of those glass ones in the middle of a bigger room on the top floor. They both walked in, produced their ID, and were escorted in by a man they did not know, who was wearing a suit and tie. It was a simply made-up room, with no desk, no cameras, only three chairs. They sat down and waited. Xantha came up the stairs from the opposite side of the room with an older man in tow. They were talking, but neither Saul nor Tom could hear them, and then Xantha nodded, took a stack of folders, and the older man left. Xantha walked toward the glass room, opened the door, and sat in the remaining chair. It was just the three of them in the room, and they all sat facing each other and waited.

There was a silence, as everyone one began to size each other up. Tommy and Saul seemed to know vaguely who Xantha was, but Xantha knew *exactly* who Saul and Tommy were. The silence continued, as Xantha crossed her legs and placed her stack of folders on her lap. One minute. Five minutes. Seven minutes passed, and no one said a word. Finally, at ten minutes exactly, Xantha spoke.

"Excellent," she said matter-of-factly. "I knew that I chose correctly."

Saul and Tom looked at each other, then at Xantha, who continued.

"I don't want a bunch of chatty Cathies who have to know everything. You were confident enough to know that the very fact that I called you both here was enough." She smiled and waited a beat. "Fantastic, really. I'm very pleased." She leaned back in her chair and asked a question. "Do either of you know why you are here?"

Saul and Tommy both slowly shook their heads.

"Good," Xantha said. "I also don't like people who have to descend to supposition and guess as to the answer to a question when they clearly have no evidence to support whatever answer they may have conjured in their heads." Xantha leaned in. "Let's just say, the reason that you are here is because I want you both to be part of something very special."

She continued. "I have been observing both of you, along with a handful of others, to see if you have what it takes. I have seen that you both possess a special group of skills, and these skills are going to allow you to have a special group of privileges." She slid her chair closer to both these men, slapped both of them on their legs, and said, "We'll definite-ly be in touch." Xantha stood to leave. Over her shoulder, as she opened the exit, she spoke one last time. "You've both gotten through the door; let's see what you do on this side of it."

Saul and Tommy watched Xantha leave, rejoin her old man friend, give him back the stack of folders, and descend the staircase that she came up, all while never looking back at either of them. She got what she wanted, they supposed, and now she was on to something else.

"I wonder what was in those folders," Tommy asked aloud.

Saul answered. "My guess is . . . nothing."

They looked at each other and smirked, and they rose out of their chairs and left. Some might have thought that this entire "meeting" was bizarre, but not Saul and Tom. And that's probably why they were chosen in the first place.

7

Three weeks earlier, Xantha had been called mysteriously into an office she had never seen before, in a building that she did not know existed. Roger had set up the meeting after forwarding Xantha's dissertation, entitled *The Program*, to the proper agents. Her thesis had first intrigued Roger and then some other higher-ups in the Agency that he had shown it to. God knows who those people worked for, but the point was that Xantha had written about some pretty provocative and progressive ideas, and these people wanted to pick her brain as to how she thought she might implement them.

At least, that is what Roger had told Xantha. Xantha was intelligent enough to know that there was something else in play at this point, but she also felt that she was smart enough to not ask any questions. Roger had contacted Xantha, pulled her aside to explain what she could expect in her upcoming meeting, and then let her be. Roger didn't want to compromise or contaminate the process that was about to unfold, but he also didn't think it was fair to just throw Xantha to the wolves either. Simply put, Roger said that these people were going to ask straight questions, so she should give straight answers.

"Should you feel the need to speak, just tell them what you think," he said. "Don't guess as to what they want to hear."

Now Xantha sat in the room where, three weeks from now, she would be questioning Saul and Tommy. She was more anxious than fearful. In fact, she remarked to herself how absolutely thrilling this was all becoming, and she allowed herself to smile a bit. Then the glass door opened and two men and one woman walked through, all three dressed in their best suits. Xantha commended herself internally for wearing her best outfit as well, and she was confident enough to stand up and extend her hand. The first man grabbed it and shook it with strength while introducing himself.

"Good morning Xantha. My name is . . . well . . . you can call me Agent Smith."

Xantha nodded, then looked to the other two people in the room.

Agent Smith looked over his own shoulder at them, then proclaimed that the other man was an FBI agent and the woman was NSA. Others from Interpol and MI6 were going to be briefed about this later, Agent Smith said.

The moment in time had slowed down for Xantha right at that moment: Did she hear correctly? Was the entire intelligence community of the Western Hemisphere to be briefed as to what happens here right now? Perhaps about what she wrote?

As if sensing her surprise, Agent Smith smiled politely and revealed, "Since 9/11, every agency gets a low-level briefing when any type of intelligence is discussed, even if it's just about potential policy shifts or best practice methods." Agent Smith finished by saying, matter-of-factly, "The intelligence community is quietly the largest community in the civilized world. There are no secrets."

While the three agents had a table to sit at, Xantha was given a single chair, placed about eight feet away from them. Agent Smith opened a folder in front of him, yet had no pen to write with. The other two agents were simply looking at Xantha, with no folder or pen.

Xantha remained cool and collected, aware of this particular tactic. It was Interrogation 101. One person asked open-ended questions, while the others looked mostly for reactions. Weaknesses, really. The others looked for weaknesses. Body language, pantomimes, breathing, physical changes, and both language and word choice were all being observed, and she knew it. One could easily become paralyzed when they know that they are under this type of surveillance, and they'd be held hostage in some way as they try to search for the safe way out.

"Before we begin, we want you to know that everyone in this room has read your thesis. All sixty-five pages. Every word," Agent Smith shifted in his seat.

And Xantha took note of that. She was surveilling them too.

"But, even with what you have laid out in your paper, there are still . . . gaps." Agent Smith waited a moment. And still another. "Do you understand?" The other two agents sat motionless, yet all eyes were on Xantha.

Xantha moved not an inch, said not a word. *Her* eyes were fixed on Agent Smith. She did not blink, but squinted very slowly as she tilted her head. Silence permeated the room, although it was not uncomfortable. Xantha was trying to ascertain whether these three were telling the truth about reading her paper. And Xantha tried to ascertain what was meant by the use of the word "gaps." *Gaps in what?* she wondered to herself. The quietness was growing.

Agent Smith broke the silence.

"You see, Xantha. We all . . . can see where you are coming from with the scenarios that you have laid out in your thesis." No other information was forthcoming by Agent Smith. He was being very deliberate and cautious with his word choice. Clearly, being careful with his words was a tactic, and Agent Smith seemed to be doing a great deal of posturing as well.

All three agents appeared to be throwing out their fishing lines to see what it is that they can snag. Not catch, but snag. They were clearly hoping to foul hook some information from Xantha, but she wasn't biting.

Xantha allowed herself to cross her legs, but still said nothing. Then she smiled. And smirked. And, quietly, let a slight one syllable laugh escape from her lips.

This made Agent Smith recoil, and the other two agents look at each other in wonderment. They then looked back at Xantha.

And did Xantha dare to see . . . fear? In the faces of these three agents? Was this the best that the intelligence community had to offer? Or was she *truly* . . . surprising them with her reactions?

Xantha squinted her eyes again, crossed her arms, and

spoke for the first time. "Where is Roger?" she asked.

The three agents looked at each other, exhaled, adjusted themselves in their chairs, and repositioned themselves.

"Look," Agent Smith began. "We're just talking here. We just want some insight into what you would propose to do. Filling these aforementioned . . . gaps." He paused, then continued. "If these ideas, and this thesis . . . achieve higher status."

Undeterred, Xantha asked again. "Where is Roger?" She waited for an answer and then stated quite firmly, "Produce him immediately, no discussion."

The agents all looked at each other, appearing to honestly not know what to do next.

Xantha stood up forcefully, kicking her chair back slightly so it scraped on the floor, making a loud noise. This got their attention. She decided to go for it and made an unconditional demand.

"You will produce Roger Bajor *right now*, or I am *leaving . . . right now*."

Xantha became incredulous at the lack of movement at this point. Still standing, she reached into her back pocket to produce her cell phone to call Roger.

All three agents stood at once, with the woman procuring a weapon, pointing it at Xantha. The other two agents put out their hands as if to say "whoa, whoa" to Xantha, and she got the message.

Moving not a muscle, Xantha said, "I'm just getting my cell phone."

Agent Smith calmly said, "I need to see your hands, please. Your phone, should that *really* be what you are going for, won't work in here. This is a safe room, and all electronic devices are neutralized the second you walk in here. Now, please, let me see your hands."

Xantha took her fingers off, then her hands, and placed them, palms out, in front of her.

The woman continued to aim her weapon at her as the conversation continued.

"Why do you want to see RED Agent Bajor?" There was fear in Agent Smith's voice, which seemed very peculiar to Xantha.

She understood the general fear of her, for she was essentially an unknown quantity. But "RED" agent? She shuffled quickly through the jargon in her head as to what that might mean. *RED* . . . she thought to herself. RED. Then she got it. Retired: Extremely Dangerous.

Without revealing anything to her current safe room occupants, Xantha's inner attitude seemed to change. She went from being interested in what this whole thing was about, to being wildly fascinated in how this was all going to end.

"Let's all just calm down," Xantha began again, as she slowly, hands raised, sat down in her chair. "Calm . . . calm. I'm sitting. I'm sitting."

The woman slowly lowered her weapon, and everyone slowly returned to their seats. There was a moment of readjustment as everyone tried to go back to square one, but it seemed that this was impossible.

Conceding that this meeting was over in some way, the two agents not called Smith got up and left the room without speaking. They seemed to march out, as if they were military, one holding the door for the other, which Xantha also noted.

Agent Smith remained as he closed his folder and spoke, "Contrary to what you might think, this meeting went better than I could have possibly hoped."

With that, Agent Smith rose, turned, and also seemed to march out of the room, leaving Xantha alone in her chair to ponder what had just happened.

In the aloneness of the room, Xantha once again smirked in her chair as she said to no one in particular, "That paper hit a nerve, huh?"

Then she stood, turned to walk out, and said, "They're scared of my friendship with Roger . . . interesting."

As soon as Xantha left the room and went out into the street, she called Roger.

When he answered, Roger quickly said, "Don't talk. Don't say anything. Just meet me at the place we discussed." Roger quickly hung up without Xantha saying a word.

One hour later, Xantha found Roger sitting on the park bench they agreed on, and she sat down next to him.

Roger, without saying one word, conveyed an impressive amount of pride in his *de facto* pupil. He smiled, nodded, and leaned in. "Your paper scared them. I couldn't tell you that, but I figured you would be able to gather that on your own with a face-to-face meeting."

Xantha smiled too. "I get it, but . . . why are they scared? I mean, I want what they want, right?"

Roger hesitated so as to put it into the right words. Then, he spoke.

"They're scared because your paper is perfect. It places their thoughts into a narrative that might actually be successful. It's airtight. And, if executed properly, it solves a lot of problems and essentially changes the world." Roger waited a beat. "For them, at least.

"You could be the mental architect that they have been

waiting for. This had to show itself organically, without any contamination, and, I'll tell you something, we might finally be there."

Roger rose from the bench.

"Get some sleep. We'll talk tomorrow about putting together the world's smallest team. Think of some people that you can trust, and get ready to grill them the way you were today."

Roger turned to walk away.

"Roger!" Xantha called out, making him turn around. "Just so you know, Sandra was great today." Xantha then cringed a little. "There weren't any bullets in that gun, was there?"

Roger shrugged, "Maybe, just in case that meeting went sideways." He smiled and added, "But, rest assured, those bullets weren't ever meant for you."

Roger winked and went on his way.

8

There are very few games like it, that much is certain. In fact, one could easily argue that there is *no* game like it. No sport, puzzle, test, and board game that are, in any way shape or form, like it. The game is meant for naturals, but it takes years to even master its basic maneuvers—and even *that* guarantees nothing at all. Should you, in fact, dominate the nuances of it, victory is never assured. One false step, one false move, one devastating mistake—and all is over.

Conversely, good fortune—and, for lack of a better word, luck—has its place within this game as well. Some have gone a long way on "all luck, no talent," but even that runs out eventually, and it's usually not pretty. In fact, it's almost always catastrophic and ultimately fatal on some level. There's just too much at stake almost all the time, and the game is just not for the faint of heart.

Texas Hold'em Poker. It is this particular game of poker that serves to define us all at some point. Clearly, it stands as a tremendous test of nearly every facet of humanity. One must be tough enough to endure the earth-shattering defeats that inevitably come to every player, and one must also be humble enough to endure the soul-crushing victories that one lays out upon his opponent. Many players recall with remarkable accuracy the devastating bad beats that they have endured, while forgetting with equally remarkable ease the pots they have taken with brutally poor play, only to be rewarded in the end by sheer dumb luck.

One of the most upsetting elements of playing Texas Hold'em is that the player can play a hand perfectly and still lose. No other sport or skill can say that about itself, yet, with the confines of this poker game, it happens all too often. It is distressing as to how much luck plays into its final outcome, but, in the end, it is the hands that you fold that, ultimately, defines you as a player.

Good Hold'em players fold their hands over 85 percent of the time and, within that statistic, over 40 percent of those folded hands end up being winners. If one begins to even *think* about that filthy statistic, one's head begins to seriously hurt.

Xantha knew how to play poker. She always said that she didn't remember not knowing how to read, didn't remember not knowing how to write, and didn't remember not knowing how to play poker. She was able to use the tools she honed as a poker player into having the innate ability to read people. She just seemed to have a sixth sense about it, and that trait has always served her well.

She knew from that first moment she saw Saul protect Tommy that day that both of those men were going to be assets to her one day. She saw the loyalty of Saul and the logic and negotiation ability of Tommy. She knew to put Sandra in the room at the meeting, which was set up by her other friend Roger, whom she had known since grade school. She knew that her paper was going to cause a stir—to hit certain nerves—but in the exact way she had hoped. She knew she was right about the government, society, and how fed up the civilized world was with the uncivil element within it. And she knew that she was on the cusp of something remarkable.

After Roger had left her on the bench, Xantha immediately got to work. She called Tommy. She called Saul. She told them both to meet her in the conference room that she had just left at 10:00 p.m. in exactly two weeks, when finals ended.

"Bring your ID, and make sure you're together, because this is going to be a joint interview."

She remarked to herself that neither Saul nor Tommy asked what this meeting was going to be about, and that boded well for both of them. Once again, she had read her adversaries well, and she knew it.

"There is something immoral about not following your instincts," Xantha had always said. And she knew she was right. She also knew that of the many imprisonments possible in our world, one of the worst was to be inarticulate—to be unable to tell another person what you really feel, or what is really going on. She knew that she would have to play that card, but only for a little while longer.

Xantha had played her hand perfectly in the meeting. So much so that she had obtained a meeting of her own, and her Program was going to go forward. She just needed to pick her team—her small team, her team of special people who will have special privileges—and then she and Roger could talk about funding. Incredibly, it was all coming together at just the right time, under just the right circumstances. For there was a political chill in the air this month, and the missing piece was about to fall into place.

His name was Clifford Crumb, and he was the world's biggest nobody. He would always clarify his last name by saying "Crumb, as in 'cake,' which I will eat too."

His enemies latched onto that by altering it and saying, "Yeah, Crumb, as in 'cake,' which he will eat *two*."

Being thin-skinned, Clifford didn't particularly like that, but he also understood that you can't choose your name. "So I guess I'm stuck being a billionaire Crumb."

Having inherited his money at the age of twenty-four from his horribly rich father, Clifford went to work, purchasing all of the real estate that $250 million could by. He took out loans, bought casinos, and would then bankrupt them by using the law as a blunt tool to get out from under the debt he would accrue through the ownership of such risky enterprises. He did this over and over again, and he would always say that those with a conscience need not apply to his business adventures.

When he was asked about his own conscience, he would say, "I had mine removed at birth."

Slowly, through default, forgiveness, and money laundering schemes, Clifford turned $250 million into more than $500 million in just over twenty-five years.

A tactic that he made the most of was the ability to run up debt under a company that he would found, and then have that company go under as he pillaged every liquid cent he could wring out of it.

He would also create false foundations that never performed any of the tasks that he said they would, and he would funnel his money through these companies, thereby saving himself millions in taxes.

Indeed, one year his companies had performed so "poorly" that he took a more than $420 million loss on all of his assets, thereby securing not only a hefty refund, but a debit that he could place up against any profits that he would incur, thereby receiving even *more* disposable income.

Clifford continued to do this over and over and put his name on almost anything and everything that he could for those hectic twenty-five years as he consolidated his empire. Clifford always pushed the envelope as to what was legal or illegal, and he clearly had no inhibitions about shedding both responsibility and morals as he financially ransacked virtually everything he touched. It seemed that Clifford simply had no problem at all using laws to increase his fortune. He did not consider what one should or shouldn't do in the moral sense, only what one could or couldn't do in the legal sense.

Clifford had no friends, only lawyers. Lots and lots of lawyers. He married three women, but he had only two children. With his first wife, a daughter—a stone-cold killer, just like her father—and with his last wife, a young son, who was essentially in absentia. That was fine with Clifford, since he adored his beautiful daughter, and he was nowhere to be found with his son.

Clifford's climb from being a shrewd and awful businessman to being a relevant politician was fast and furious indeed. Mostly considered a buffoon by his political peers, he was considered a savior of sorts by those desperate to maintain the status quo—a man they could count on to be a horrible man. Clifford had no respect for others who did not think, feel, act, or look like him, and he was completely surprised (and mildly amused) at how many people felt the same way. Indeed, there were more of these people than one would think, and it was the "perfect storm" of sorts the world had not seen since the days of Mussolini, Stalin, and Hitler.

"I wouldn't call myself a dictator, per se," Clifford would postulate. "More of an opportunist. And if a dictatorship comes with that, then so be it." Clifford would constantly antagonize, poke, and prod both the press and the people around him just to get a rise out of them. A firm believer in the axiom, "There's no such thing as bad press," Crumb would push the envelope in this fashion as well. Indeed, it seemed that Clifford thrived on the talent of saying something that he knew would upset people.

And now, here he was, being thought of as someone who could run the nation. Or, at least, someone who should become the leader of the nation, one who could be manipulated and massaged into being exactly what "they" wanted him to be, whoever "they" were. Indeed, once the Cold War ended and the intelligence community had to "pick up their marbles and go home," that same community had to look for another enemy to live and die for. They found that enemy domestically, and they also quietly found a citizenry that agreed with them. The Dead Wood, as Clifford would constantly call them. Those who did nothing to further either the well-being of the nation or the financial health of the same.

"If you're not consuming, then you're not helping," Clifford would often say. "And we have to get rid of those who are not helping."

Clifford had, unbeknownst to almost anyone who knew

him, marveled at the power and the glory of being a political leader. Books were written about them. People loved them or hated them. Remarkably, Crumb didn't care which category he fell into. He just yearned to be important. In fact, as he was moving through his thirties and forties, if he was particularly bored some days, he would call some reporter or editor that he knew and give them a sound bite that they could print. It made for entertaining watercooler talk, but it also laid the groundwork for just how tolerant people would be of him. It also showed just how much people would put up with from him and also how much the world would underestimate him.

Clifford was always impressed with one event in particular that he was able to safely witness from afar. A tremendous hurricane had absolutely devastated a city in the south, and Clifford watched with amazement at how little the general public seemed to care about the people who were affected, and how much people seemed to care about the power of one of nature's most amazing spectacles. People would be overcome by the physical devastation of before and after pictures of these events, yet they asked not one word as to the well-being of the citizens impacted. No one cared about the people, because from a psychological standpoint, they weren't them, so they didn't care.

Clifford also noticed that those who were in power at the time just left these affected people to their fate. And he realized one reason was because the people being affected were incredibly poor. This state had the highest unemployment rate, crime rate, and homelessness rate in the entire country. These were people who "were living off of the government tit" and were not consuming at the rate necessary to be considered a good capitalist citizen. And Clifford remarked that most people agreed with that sentiment, even though he had no evidence to back that sentiment up. It just sounded true, and felt true, so it must be true as far as Crumb was concerned.

Clifford had come to the political game very late. And that only served to help his cause, since he was to be viewed as an outsider—not someone who was a career politician, or even a very slight politician. He was a breath of fresh air, as his constituents would have you believe. And for a very short while, he was.

His mild upset victory in the presidential election two years previous surprised even Clifford, but he would never admit that openly. Being someone who was unfamiliar with how Washington worked, he surrounded himself with a group of people who could show him the ropes politically, and for a while, people got over the fact that he was the president. But in a cunning and brilliant move, Clifford slowly pared away these people and replaced them with "yes men" who simply did whatever he asked of them and followed him without question.

Crumb was able to appoint sympathetic court judges, two Supreme Court justices, and replace or fire nearly all of the heads of every intelligence agency. He went down the line of a host of ambassadors, advisors, and previously unknown acquaintances of his from the old days so that, about halfway through his elected term, he had everyone in place to do almost anything he wanted, right or wrong.

It was within this particular light that an idea such as Xantha's could take root. A simple, yet controversial idea that would require quiet funding: a small, elite group and a clandestine platform that would protect higher-ups should The Program go either sideways or completely off the rails. In any case, it was the perfect storm of sorts that smacked of the "Kansas City Shuffle." Clifford made the whole world look "over here," while Xantha (with Roger's help) could install her Program "over there."

Before anyone knew what was even happening in the intelligence community, the groundwork was being laid for a splinter package that was going to be difficult to remove once it was in place.

Xantha was very proud of what she had accomplished. She had enlisted the help of a well-known asset (Roger), procured a meeting with a group of heads of agencies to successfully feel them out as to what they thought, and had gotten the go-ahead to form a team. All of this without raising any alarms at all as to what she was potentially up to.

She had successfully found herself with a substantial chip stack in the game of poker that was the intelligence community. She had grinded out a few questionable hands, and she had forced others to reveal their own without so much as a whimper. And, over the course of the next few months, she would slowly win the confidence of several key talents and the trust of all who were involved. And Xantha was more than confident that once she could show unquestionable results, she would be able to turn those who would object into true believers themselves.

But she had to move fast and bat 1.000 immediately—or it would all fade away, like so much mist on a cool autumn's day.

9

It was a day like any other, except this was the day that Xantha went before the four heads of the intelligence community to—at last—convince them of the wisdom of her Program. So for her, this was the first day of the rest of her life. As she bounded up the stairs of the committee room and into the soundproof antechamber of CIA office, she marveled at how far she had come in just eight short months. Saul and Thomas were to be with her, and she was going to be supported by Roger should the need arise. But it was made very clear to her that she was the one who was to do the talking. For this was her idea, and who would know more about the intricacies of the most concise idea ever to hit the intelligence community in more than twenty years?

Xantha remembered what Roger had told her all those months ago: "They are going to ask you straight questions, so give them straight answers." She took a deep breath, briefcase in hand, and opened to door to her destiny.

Xantha took her seat, and Saul and Tommy were already there at a table behind her, while Roger was off to the side in the front row. As she sat at her table, surrounded but alone, she noticed that there were microphones, but no recording devices. The room was well lit, but there were no cameras. And there were many black windows, but only three people there to question her. She gathered that the black windows were one-way mirrors, so she knew others were watching and listening, but no one was going to be on the record. She became thrilled at what was about to happen and no longer feared for her life. *If I am to be killed*, she thought, *then I can think of no greater place to go to my grave.* She finished the thought in her head. *This is fine.* And with that sentiment, it began.

"We are here today to surmise whether this ambitious conglomeration of the intelligence community, coupled with private and outside assistance, should move forward," one of the three men calmly stated. "After a considerable amount of time, and an equally considerable amount of effort, it has come to the attention of this community that, frankly, we should hear you out.

"There are still many questions here today that I hope will at least begin to be answered, but this panel sees no reason why, at the end of the day, this endeavor should not be entertained."

The three men looked at each other, and then the middleman spoke into his microphone, simply saying, "Okay. Let's begin."

Xantha began in an extremely calculated manner. She wondered to herself, *Is there something I could say that would scare these guys off?* After thinking about it for a moment, she concluded, *No. This is it. Tell them what you think.*

So she did.

"Gentlemen, we are here today because those who make up our society have let us down." She took a sip of water and continued. "In play here is a social contract that has been betrayed and broken, and we should no longer try to fix it. Instead, let us all try to move past it, and be better in the passing. Now, what I propose may seem radical, or it may seem progressive. It may make you recoil in horror or move closer so that you can hear more. But what it undoubtedly is . . . is different.

"There are those who continue to take advantage of our civility. Yours and mine. But we cannot ignore the fact that what *we* want is what *you* want. We want this world and this country to run right. And if that means that we all must begin to not just think 'outside the box,' but think as if there *is* no box, then so be it.

"The proposal put before you is fair, equitable, and just. These people who we will go after have been given more than enough time, money, and energy to either change their ways or reveal the fact that they will not alter their behavior or their values. Ever. Whatever you decide to do, please bear in mind . . . please *remember* always . . . this *absolute truth* . . . that these people, whatever happens next, have done this to themselves. Enough is enough, gentlemen, and it is *time*."

Xantha looked up from her prepared statements, looked at each one of her three listeners up on the dais in the eye, and closed her file. Slowly, she stood up and prepared to speak. She could see Roger shuffling uncomfortably in his chair, worried about what she would say next. Roger conceded in his mind that Xantha knew what she was doing and, in fact, was about to do what he had always told her to do: tell them what she thinks. So she did. She earned this moment.

"There is a pestilence that has permeated the very soul of this planet. Now, I can only do something about this country, but the long-term vision is that, should this Program work *here*, then perhaps it could work everywhere, no matter what the government, no matter what the rhetoric, no matter who the leaders are."

She began to lay out here case. "Every year, people have their lives forever altered through no fault of their own. Every moment, this nation has horrible tragedy and despair intermittently woven into its fabric by terrible, awful people committing the most atrocious of crimes. And every year, we—as a nation—turn a blind eye."

She began to move from behind her table so she could get closer to those whom she was desperately trying to sway. "Fine!" Xantha exclaimed. "This nation wants to turn a blind eye? Let them! But I will not—and this government should not either," Xantha continued.

"Forget the moral questions that are in play here." She said it again, "Forget them! Forget also the logistics around this issue. Forget the logistics, the difficulty, and the initial investment of both money and men. Instead, look at the end game." She paused for effect, and then continued. "There are two extremely important elements in play here that *demand* something be done."

Xantha paused for effect, then went on. "Should you choose to fund this Program, then we—as a nation, together—will be removing the most horrific, dreadful, draining, and appalling aspects of both this nation and this world from sight. *And* we will be creating and saving revenue by doing it."

That last statement made all three of her evaluators shift a little in their seats, as they all leaned forward in an unconscious maneuver that indicated interest. Xantha noticed this, was encouraged, and went on. "Remove those who look to harm our people, and create a safer, more lucrative society in the removing.

"Endorse this Program. *Fund* this Program. Embrace this Program, and you will secure the *future* both of this *nation* and its citizens who *matter*."

Xantha was about to continue, but one of the mediators raised his hand to stop her and then waved her forward to him so they could speak. Xantha strode to the bench and listened to what he said. "You have made your case, and it is without a doubt, *compelling*. But come with me a moment, so we can talk some more."

Xantha followed him to an antechamber behind their bench, closing the door behind him. He turned to her to speak. "This Program is fantastic. How did you come up with it?"

Xantha hesitated before responding, and then did not say anything.

Seeing her apprehension, he continued, "I understand your hesitation to speak about this, but you need to know that you are among friends here." He shook his head and asked again, "I just have to know . . . where did this idea come from?"

Xantha began to speak, then saw the table in the room and motioned for both of them to sit down, which they did. She took a deep breath, not wanting to leave anything out but wanting her answer to be as comprehensive as possible.

"Sir, I need to tell you a story. A story about the history of this great nation."

He nodded to her as if to indicate that she may proceed, so she did.

"Sometime in the past, this nation was deeply divided by many issues, most importantly, about what role we were to play. People who supported our last war were fond of saying 'My country: right or wrong.' Or 'My nation: love it or leave it.'" She stopped for a moment to make eye contact. "That sentiment seemed insane to me. We don't want to live in a country that we're going to support whether it's right or wrong no matter what. We want to live in a country that acts rightly and doesn't act wrongly."

Xantha then said something that was mildly surprising, but encapsulated her true sentiment. "What you and I feel is 'right' is the only thing that matters from here on in," she continued.

"Sir, our country isn't doing that, and it needs to be corrected. This nation has a group of people with very different ideas of what patriotism means. Personally, the flaw within this nation is that we continue to give those who have not earned it second, third, and fourth chances, while those who are both law-abiding and what I consider patriotic are left by the wayside to fend for themselves." Xantha tied up her thought. "So, you see, this nation began an era many years ago in which two groups of people—both thinking that they were acting patriotically—went to war with each other. This war is tearing this nation apart, and I will no longer stand idly by and watch from the sidelines," Xantha continued.

"Sir, I am a student of history. Since as long as I can remember, I have been so. And I have also been a firm believer that if you have a problem—any problem—you can always find a solution if you are brave enough to not only *see* it but also execute that solution." Xantha could see that her explanation was landing well, so she continued. "If you can look at a problem objectively and without emotion, you can always boil it down to one or two issues that will inevitably reveal themselves to be a solution that is viable."

"If you are brave enough to see it," her newfound friend parroted back at her.

"And also brave enough to *do* it," she reminded.

He nodded as if to say to her, "Go on," so she did.

"The enormity of the problems that seem to present themselves on a daily basis in this world always seem to have the caveat of money and funding attached to them. In short, we throw *gobs* of money at the problems and hope they are solved.

"That hasn't worked so far, and I doubt that will work in the future. In fact, the problems just seem to get worse." Xantha was ready to bring it home, so she took one more deep breath. "I see what no one else does." She paused, then continued. "What I see *works*. Finally, at long last, a solution presented itself to me several years ago, and it is this: the mechanism of society is broken, and that mechanism is one of trust. And faith.

"We can no longer trust this society to behave itself with no guidance. We no longer have the faith necessary believe that we as a civilization will improve without drastic intervention." Xantha paused for a moment, then relented. "I mean, how many opportunities are we going to give society to correct itself?" Xantha brought her point home. "That is where my Program comes in."

Then Xantha did something that she didn't plan on, but she did it anyway, out of pure emotion. She grabbed him by the shoulders, pulled him in close, and said something expressive, desperate, and perfectly timed. "Why can't anyone see that a terrible event can lead to something wonderful?" She looked into his eyes to see if he could understand her. "Help me . . . come with me . . . we'll build it together. We are only moments away from my—our—*destiny*!" She held him close, looked in his eyes, and saw consent and approval. "Will you help me save this country?"

Taking in both the passion and the logic standing in front of him, he slowly nodded, hypnotized by her desire and won over by her commitment. Still being held, he said to her, "You've got your funding. All of it. Money, equipment, a charter, an opening group, and even a black site if you want it. It's yours. Meet me with Roger on Monday at my office."

Trying desperately to hide her elation, she released him.

He straightened his clothing, smiled, and turned to leave the room. "You opened this door, Miss Grasso. Let's see what we can both do on this side of it."

Xantha waited a moment and then followed him, re-entering the chamber where this all began, and then went back to her seat.

Sitting once more at his bench with the other two men, he completed his task. "I see no need for further discussion. This Program has been approved and will move to the next stage of development to be determined at a later date. We stand adjourned." He slammed a gavel, and the three men rose and left.

Thomas, Saul, and Roger approached Xantha, and there were muted handshakes all around. It had been a long road, to say the least, and they could not have been more satisfied.

Saul had to ask about the elephant in the room. "What

did you *say* back there?"

Xantha smiled and said, "I told him the truth. That The Program is this nation's only hope." And the Xantha went one step further. "And he agreed with me."

"He said that?" Thomas said.

Xantha looked at both men and concluded, "He didn't have to. He knows that some people have earned the pain that they are receiving. I get the sense that he *always* knew at least *that* was true, and he just needed someone like me. to come along and say it." Xantha finished by saying, "I think he understands . . . whatever happens next, these people that we are going after? They did it to themselves."

She started to walk away, then looked back over her shoulder and said something wildly devastating and remarkably true, as far as she was concerned. "If you have to kill one person to cure cancer . . . wouldn't you have to do that?" And then she walked out, closing the door behind her, victorious in her quest. It was, as she would say later, the end of the beginning.

And just like that, after a long and arduous battle of wills, intellect, philosophy, and a desperate need for leadership, The Program—and the CRP—was born.

10

It was happening again. Saul came home and collapsed on his couch, exhausted from the stress of the day. The successful launch of The Program earlier had been much more fatiguing than he had realized, along with a nagging process that flowed through his brain that convinced him that he was right. And he fell asleep. A deep, unending sleep that he so clearly needed.

And it was happening again.

Only hours before, Saul had witnessed the most spectacular thing he had seen in his entire life: Xantha convincing a politician to spend vast amounts of money on what appeared to be an unproven program borne out of the mind of an untried asset. Saul had a feeling wash over him that his victory was nearly complete. He had truly found his purpose in life. And he could now rest the sleep of the righteous. And he began to dream. And not just any dream, but The Dream.

Since Saul was an eleven-year-old boy, for some reason,

he had a particularly savage recurring dream that would show itself every now and again. And after dreaming this dream, Saul would awake to a type of sleep paralysis, causing wild amounts of stress and fear upon waking and also being so severe that—for a time—Saul sought therapy for it. During his therapy sessions, Saul would try to explain the nature of this dream.

His psychologist, Dr. Steven Todd, was a patient man, who took the long way around in Saul's hour-long, weekly sessions. First, Dr. Todd would ask Saul about his week. That was essentially an icebreaker of sorts, beginning with the wildly benign question, "So how's it going?"

Saul was eleven, and he loved to talk. To his credit, Saul did not resist therapy the way that some his age (or not) usually did. To Saul, therapy was not invasive, meaningless, or, in any way, something to be avoided. Indeed, Saul always felt best at the end of his sessions and, in truth, could not wait for the next session to start.

Knowing that Dr. Todd was going to ask, Saul made many mental and physical notes of all of the emotions he was feeling during said week. And knowing that "honesty is the best policy," Saul would endeavor to be as honest with himself as he possibly could.

"You get out of it what you put into it," Dr. Todd would always say. "We can learn as much or as little as you want to about yourself during these sessions. Personally, I hope you choose to learn a lot. That will only be a good thing."

Dr. Todd resisted point-blank asking Saul about the dream that was dominating him and, instead, would gather information through his "talk therapy." Dr. Todd would be honest with Saul, explaining to him that eventually they would have to confront his particular dream, but how in the meantime, they would build a foundation of trust through talking about virtually anything.

Dr. Todd, as he would convey, was a student of all philosophy and a particular fan of two adages. One was Sigmund Freud's belief that "dreams are wishes." The other axiom was that "one sometimes only knows that they are dreaming when they wake up." Dr. Todd explained that this last one was part of something called "lucid dreaming" and made clear that this was a tactic he was going to make use of with Saul.

After several sessions, Dr. Todd asked Saul to not only take notes—both mentally and otherwise—about his week, but also about the dreams he might have. "Keep a notepad next to your bed, and write down whatever you can the moment you wake up.

"Now, be aware," Dr. Todd cautioned, "if and when you read that notepad later, it may make no sense at all. In fact, that actually happens quite often. But don't be discouraged. In the end, this tactic usually bears fruit."

Probably because of the fact that the therapy was having the desired effect, Saul went a few weeks without having the dream that sent him to therapy in the first place. But that ended one evening, about six weeks into his treatment. And it seemed to come back with a vengeance.

The dream always seemed to start the same: it was dark, there was a large crowd of faceless people who were quietly moaning, lightning was flashing, but there was no thunder. And it was as if an enormous storm was about to begin but was forever stalled. And there was always something else. It was difficult to explain, as are all dreams that are not one's own: there was a creature: not good, not bad, just . . . there. And it was always warm. Humid and warm.

The creature would always be behind the faceless group of people, and those people stretched the entire horizon. The lightning flashed like heat lightning, brightening the entire sky for a split second, allowing Saul to see the face of the creature for just a moment. There were horns, eyeless sockets, and a mouth that seemed to have fire simmering within it. The creature then stepped over, on, and through the crowd. Always toward Saul, with purpose. Saul was paralyzed within his dream, powerless to stop it or interact with it. The creature waved its demon arms at Saul, trying to either strike him or capture him. Saul was always successful in avoiding contact, and he would always sort of stumble backward and fall on his backside. The creature breathed deep and prepared to expel flame and fire from its mouth. And then Saul would wake up. Every time, at that moment, Saul would awaken. Scared, paralyzed with fear, and experiencing shortness of breath. And that was the dream.

Saul was simply scared of it, but Dr. Todd was beyond impressed with the details, including the sound, sight, and sense of touch. Dr. Todd remarked about both the colors and the imagery in play, and he was confident that he could help.

Over the next weeks and months, Dr. Todd and Saul would work tirelessly with each other. Saul would document his week, and Dr. Todd would educate Saul about what his dreams meant, and what the surrounding therapy could do to help improve Saul's life going forward. Finally, fulfilling his promise, Dr. Todd began to teach Saul about "lucid dreaming."

"Lucid dreaming," Dr. Todd would say, "happens when you're aware that you're dreaming. Often, you can control the dream's storyline and environment. It occurs during REM sleep. When used in therapy, like we are doing, lucid dreaming can help treat conditions like your recurring nightmare."

Saul understood, and for the next few sessions, Dr. Todd would give Saul tools to apply to not only this particular nightmare but also *all* dreams. And the tools worked.

Saul was already using a "dream journal," but other techniques revolving around testing your reality while inside the dream (like poking yourself in the palm of your hand or touching the ground around you) also began to show results.

"You judge your reality by the use of your senses. When you cannot trust your senses, there is no reality." That was an impressive attitude that Dr. Todd continued to promote and, soon, Saul was using that technique more than any other.

Saul began to realize that he could affect his dreams by recognizing that he was, in fact, dreaming. And then he would fashion items within that dream, such as a weapon or another item, to help him. Or even put to use irrational ideas, such as stopping time or rewinding what just happened. Mostly successful, but sometimes not, Saul, at least, was honing skills that were to serve him well in these situations and working to push his one nightmare into the background for good.

And then, after six months, Saul's family moved to New Jersey. It was too far for Saul to continue his therapy with Dr. Todd, and there was a general consensus that the therapy had reached its limit anyway. All was well, but Saul was disappointed. During their last session, Dr. Todd congratulated him on making exceptional progress where most had failed and encouraged him to continue enhancing the skill that they had both worked so hard to perfect.

Over the course of the next several years, Saul's therapy waned, and then he just decided that he didn't really need it anymore. Saul became a Marine and, at the age of twenty, went to study law at the University of Virginia, where he would find Thomas and Xantha.

He was so close to his purpose in life that he could barely stand it, but it seemed tantalizingly forever out of reach. Until he fell asleep on his couch. And he dreamed the dream once more. It had been a very long time, but without knowing it, Saul was ready to confront it.

He was there again, at the beginning of the storm, with the creature and the lightning. And the moaning faceless people. And the creature approached, slowly lumbering toward him. Saul knew he was dreaming and, for once, he was not afraid. He had a plan.

As the creature reached for him, Saul did something both daring and impressively aware: He allowed the creature to touch him. And as the creature made contact with its swipe, suddenly, Saul was being swept up into the air. His stomach tingled and tickled as it would in real life when one begins to gain altitude. And then the creature did something else: It began to protect him. Saul found himself behind the creature, and Saul was growing larger. And larger. And now, he was standing next to it, and he had a weapon. He was unsure as to what weapon he was holding, but suddenly, he was one with purpose. The creature took a breath, and Saul could feel the heat of its mouth. The creature exhaled toward the moaning and blasted fire from its mouth, and then Saul was firing his weapon as well. They were both working together to destroy the moaning crowd that came at them endlessly, but not threateningly. Saul and his monster were dominating now, serving a single-minded action and attitude, destroying that which was perceived to be evil. The sound was beginning to be deafening. And it was good.

Then Saul awoke with a start. The dream made sense. Finally, at long last, the dream had finished. He smiled the smile of the righteous as he had figured it out. He had ambiguously dreamed of "purpose" all those years ago, and now, he filled the gap that was this dream. It was The Program. And there was one other thing . . .

"Xantha!" he whispered aloud. "The creature is Xantha!"

11

"I need receipts" the short, balding Jewish man said in his decidedly German-American accent. "Do not forget to write on this pad that you will find inside of your own personal safe deposit box *exactly* what you take out. That will count as a receipt of funds. I do not care *what* you use the money for, just make certain that you write down the date and amount that you take out." He said his opening phrase once more for effect. "I need *receipts*."

His name was Emile Roche, and he had done this before. Indeed, when Mossad and Israel had committed themselves and their government to the hunting of Nazis post–World War II, and then to the hunting of terrorist organizations such as Black September in the '70s and '80s, people like Emile Roche were heavily involved in the clandestine financial backing and distribution of funds that were used to fight those battles, and the manner in which The Program was to be funded was no different.

The room was filled with ten operatives at a time, and for the next few weeks, one hour at a time, from 9:00 a.m. until 4:00 p.m., Emile was to give the same exact speech and guidance to each team as to how they would access their funds. "You will draw a base salary of forty-two thousand dollars that will be fully taxable and aboveboard, spread out over twenty-four payments, and that money will be paid to you on the fifteenth and twenty-eighth day of every month into an account of your choosing. But the rest of your salary will be paid to you in cash, and you will access that money through a safe deposit box that will be assigned to you, and only you." Emile paused for effect to make certain that this point that he was about to make next hit home.

"Each of your safe deposit boxes will be filled on January fifteenth of each year with $150,000 cash, which you will have access to any time your bank is open. Occasionally, you will have information dropped into your safe deposit box. Sometimes, we will communicate with you through this box, and you will communicate with us should you wish to," Emile continued.

"This government works with two financial institutions domestically: United American Bank and The Bank of the Atlantic. Both of these banks have the most branches worldwide, and they do business with every nation in the EU, plus Great Britain and Asia. You will have no problems at all doing whatever business you wish to through these banks."

Emile went on to explain how this was, quite simply, the easiest, most clandestine method of compensation for the priceless work that all of them were about to do. Emile even drifted into "the nature of the beast" and explained how each member of society had a role to play and a part to perform, and all of them, including himself, were about to do it. Calling each and every one of the ten operatives in that room receiving their preparation for duty as heroes to the cause, Emile finished by explaining that their work will never end so long as they all keep doing it. Then, he added one more thing.

Emile looked around at the ten trainee operatives in the room, came around his desk, and sat upon it. Taking a survey of the group, Emile wanted to make certain that each and every eye was on him before he began. Taking a deep breath, he started his soliloquy on justice.

"Gentlemen—and this is important—you are, quite frankly, the best of the best. You have been plucked from the choir, and now you are about to be polished like the most valuable of gems. All of you have been chosen from the most elite groups: Marines, Rangers, and Special Forces. And as elite as those groups most certainly are, the paramilitary force that we are assembling is going to be even more elite than that." Emile looked around and saw that his speech most certainly was landing. He continued.

"As you might have guessed, special soldiers get to have special privileges. As you move through this Program in the next few weeks, all of you will begin to understand what is at stake and how you are going to help." Emile stood up and turned to go back behind his desk. "In the next room, you will be told what your weapons will be and how they will be utilized to their maximum efficiency. Dismissed, gentlemen."

The ten stood as one, and they filed calmly through the door in the back of the room to their next station: weapons.

As they entered the room and sat at their desks, it was Roger that was to instruct them as to the weapons at their disposal and how the teams will be designed. But before all of that, Roger had a speech to give.

"As I'm sure you're all aware, you are all the best of the best. Handpicked by us from elite military teams: Marines, Special Forces, Rangers. All of you have what it takes, as far as we're concerned. Now, you are going to make a difference. You are all personnel with special gifts. Special gifts come with special privileges. I hope you can handle that, because you are all going to do some extraordinary work."

Roger then moved toward explaining the one and only weapon that will be at their disposal. A weapon that they all knew very well: the .32 ACP pistol with a suppressor. "Just so all of you know, ACP means automatic colt pistol. And we use the word suppressor, not silencer, when describing this weapon. Is that clear?"

A resounding "Sir, *yes sir!*" filled the room, and Roger continued.

"This is your only weapon, and you will soon see why. Many feel that the .32 is a . . . woman's pistol." Sporadic chuckles and laughs were heard. "But the .32 does the job, people. A .22 is too small, and you might have to hit your target multiple times to finish the job. Anything larger than a .32 causes too much blowback and residual data to be released.

"But the .32 is exactly the precision instrument that you will need to carry out your missions that are assigned to you."

Roger went on to explain how a team of ten will be created for each member, with three being assigned point. There will also be one driver, two bagmen, two spotters, and two disposal technicians that will eliminate the target.

"I know that these words I am saying do not mean much to you at this time, but during the course of your training, you will begin to understand them."

Roger continued to fill the hour with talk of how those who have been chosen should be very proud, and he was once like them back in the day. Roger kept hitting on the point that they all, through close observation, had been chosen not only for their physical attributes, but also for their professional ones. Just follow orders, Roger continued to say, and their jobs would be done.

After finishing his speech, Roger ushered them into the next room, where they were to meet Thomas. Thomas would reveal to them who or what their targets would be. Roger ended by guaranteeing his group that they would be extremely pleased with what Thomas was to say next.

The men moved swiftly into the next room, sat in their desks, and waited for Thomas to appear. Thomas entered from the side, dressed in a blue suit and tie, and informed the men who this Program was going after.

"The worst of the worst, gentlemen. We are targeting the worst of the worst." Thomas proceeded to tell them about the rapists, violent addicts, abusers, child murderers, and how a large part of The Program revolved around the "forever criminal."

"These are the people," Thomas would say, "that have become an excessive drain upon our society. The 'hopeless recidivist.'"

The men were to be completely on board with these targets, most would guess, but he explained the difference in this particular target group. Most, if not all, of the targets would be the "persistently criminal." Thomas would continue to explain that those that The Program would look to eliminate those who, in his words, "have shown that they are either unable or unwilling to become functioning members of society."

There was no pushback in any way on this, as most of the men nodded their approval. "We will never give you a target who has not been thoroughly vetted in every way. And you, with the training that you will receive, will make zero mistakes." Thomas then leaned in and reiterated that point, with an add-on. "You will make zero mistakes because you will be trained and drilled, as such. And one other thing: You do not exist. At all. You will be flawless because you cannot afford not to be.

"This is the elitism that we here at The Program are both promoting and insisting upon." Thomas looked around the room and made his point, "Is this, in any way, unclear?"

A resounding "Sir, *no sir*" echoed in the room.

"Outstanding."

Thomas did not reveal to the men that would enter this Program—and pass through his room—that the ones who were chosen would have other parameters attached to them. It had been long discussed that the assets within The Program were to be both unmarried (optimally, single) and all heterosexual men. Without truly discriminating, the groups of ten just simply needed to be one with their task, and adding a sexual element created a variable that would have eventually become untenable.

Not that any of the men needed convincing, but Thomas was able to parrot the theories and suppositions that Xantha had created at the genesis of this Program back at them to solidify both the urgency of this mission and the palpability of it. Thomas knew that the possibility of some of these men in this room might lose their enthusiasm for their task if they thought about it too much, so he got out ahead of any unspoken qualms they might have by being very clear about their shared goals.

"There is an enemy within this civilization that is slowly eating away at the soul of the nation we love. The nation that all of us, including myself, have signed up to protect. Stay frosty, people. Your mission is authorized, and your targets are real. You are performing your mission by eliminating these targets. I know that once you see what it is we are doing, your passion for your duty will exponentially grow.

"You men are dismissed. You will continue your training and await further instructions."

They all rose as one and left Thomas's sight for the last time. And for a variety of reasons, this was the last time any of them would ever see Thomas again. But none of them knew that.

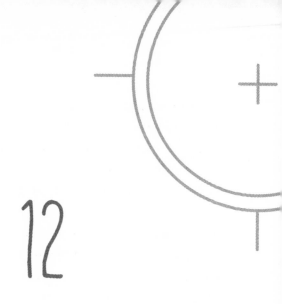

12

The Cellular Reorganization Program, or The Program for short, was a devastating idea from the devastating mind of one Xantha Grasso. Xantha based The Program heavily upon her disdain for the "barnacles of society," as she called them, and an algorithm that she had conjured from the mathematics of the human condition. Surely, others had dreamed of such a program, she correctly posited, but it was either their unconditional love for humans that got in their way or their irrational hatred of them. While all the previous creators had love for humans, Xantha only had a love for humanity. It was the human element that needed to be reckoned with and surgically cut out like the cancer that it was.

For thousands of years—Xantha had posited in her dissertation—humanity had hinged the civility that it cherished (and had placed so much value upon) on a hope that never truly revealed itself. Humanity, she claimed, was forever being held together by the thinnest of threads that was so easily broken again and again, only to be rebuilt and retied in a never-ending, futile attempt at finding order within chaos. Leadership was needed that would acknowledge the devastating reality that some of this world would have to be sacrificed to save the rest of it. Privately, Xantha prided herself on the fact that she was not held hostage by the incipient morality that had befallen nearly everyone she knew. This morality, quite simply, was in the way, as far as she was concerned, and, ultimately, it served no purpose. *That* was the devastating algorithm that Xantha had discovered all on her own, and no one could take that away from her, and it was this: not everyone was the same, and there was a specific group that was dragging society down. And society kept trying to raise these barnacles up, only to have them continue to sink the ship. With Xantha's Program, that was all going to change. But that sword clearly cut both ways.

Just because no one could take it away from her did not mean that others did not try. Xantha found that out the hard way one evening. Roger visited her that night without notice. He clearly had something to say, and he clearly wished that he had approached her about it sooner. But here he was, and it was time to come clean.

Xantha had just settled down with a glass of wine when she heard a light tapping on her apartment door. When she opened the door, she was surprised to see Roger standing there.

"May I come in?"

"Sure. Of course."

Roger entered, looked around aimlessly with his hands in his pockets, and then spun to face Xantha.

A silence permeated the room, and Xantha broke it with a simple question: "What is it Roger? What's wrong?"

Roger had that look in his eye that illustrated the fact that he had something extremely important to say (confess?), and he needed Xantha to sit down. She did. Roger sat down to face her, and then he began.

"Many years ago, when I was an active agent, I was part of another project. It was called the Phoenix Project, and its parameters were not unlike the ones that serve as the lynchpins of your Program. Phoenix was initially designed to identify and destroy certain perceived enemies by way of infiltration, torture, capture, counterterrorism, interrogation, and . . ." Roger purposefully hesitated before revealing the last tactic, "assassination." Roger went on to explain that the CIA described it as a set of programs that sought to attack and destroy the political infrastructure of any enemy. The Phoenix Project was premised on the idea that infiltration had required local support from noncombat civilian populations, which were referred to as the political branch that had purportedly coordinated the insurgency. "We needed to flip these 'political branches' to control certain elements of the enemy at the highest level."

Xantha was taking all of this in but was unsure why Roger was telling her this.

Roger went on.

"It was a long time ago, and to be honest, we did some terrible things to achieve our goals." But before Roger even got to that, he explained how Phoenix essentially worked.

The two major components of the program, Roger explained, were called the Provincial Recon Units (PRUs) and regional interrogation centers. "The PRUs would kill or capture suspected enemy members as well as civilians who were thought to have information on their activities. Many of these people were taken to interrogation centers and were tortured in an attempt to gain intelligence on enemy activities in the area," Roger went on.

"The information extracted at the centers was given to military commanders, who would use it to task the PRU with further capture and assassination missions. The program's effectiveness was measured in the number of 'enemies' who were 'neutralized,' which was a not-so-gentle euphemism that meant imprisoned, persuaded to defect and help us, or killed."

Xantha nodded and continued to listen. She was always very good at knowing when to be silent and just listen. It really was an impressive attribute.

Roger continued.

"Agencies that were used within Phoenix were the CIA, Special Forces, Navy Seals, Army intelligence officers, and certain Marines who seemed to have a natural proclivity for this type of work." Xantha nodded again, trying to keep up with what Roger was saying. "One of the central components to Phoenix is the fact that it targeted civilians, not soldiers." Roger added something else. "Civilians in *other* countries."

Xantha was beginning to see where this was going. "Roger. You don't have to worry about my Program. The only people who are going are people who no one is going to miss."

Roger nodded, and then continued.

"You think that is true, but if you're not careful, some of the people that you are neutralizing *will* be missed. And that creates nothing but trouble for everyone. In Phoenix, one of the luxuries we had in the beginning is that we could occasionally shoot and miss, but you? You can't miss. Not even once. I mean, are you prepared for that level of perfection?"

Xantha nodded and then asked a sensitive question. "What happened in Phoenix?"

Roger took a deep breath and told the story of the rise and fall of Phoenix.

"One could argue that we just got careless and cocky. I mean, initially, it was working. We were successfully taking targets who were doing real damage to the political infrastructure of the governments that we were trying to influence. But it just got too busy. Too many targets without the proper amount of vetting. Killing people that we didn't know. Allowing one bad decision to create three more issues. It just got out of hand."

Roger felt the need to tell this part of the story. "Phoenix's operations often aimed to assassinate targets or, in some cases, cause their deaths through other means. PRU units often anticipated resistance in disputed areas and often operated on a shoot-first basis. This became a fatal issue to the Phoenix Project." Roger explained that, in the end, many operatives from all levels became overzealous in the liberties that Phoenix allowed them to have simply because of the very nature of the tasks being performed. Some on the outside of the Phoenix Project talked about it as basically an assassination program that also included torture. They would also kill people by throwing them out of helicopters to threaten and intimidate those they wanted to interrogate. "Sometimes, when we marked a target, we would grab him and four of his associates. During the interrogation of the primary, we would slowly and methodically neutralize and eliminate his associates right in front of him . . . one by one."

Xantha knew what that meant, but she was unmoved.

"Inevitably, after Phoenix Project abuses began receiving negative publicity, the program was officially shut down, although it continued under the name Sky Fox or Pegasus—I really don't remember—for several more years, but without government funding, and at an incredibly reduced scale." Roger then brought his point home.

"I think that your Program has a real chance to succeed where Phoenix failed. If you can control your assets, limit your damage, and hit your targets without any collateral damage, I really think this Program can work." Roger finished his thought. "I mean, you have taken a foreign policy program that had inherent flaws within it that mostly revolved around integrity and honor, and turned it into a domestic program that maximizes itself through a laser focused purpose.

"It's one of the reasons that I came onboard. And it's the main reason why it was approved. I took your Program to people who needed redemption from the Phoenix Project, and they agreed that your Program was worth the stretch. So . . . thank you for that," Roger finally finished his point.

"It was of the utmost importance that you came to your Program organically, without any contamination from me or anyone else who know what you were up to. We threw you some curve balls in the beginning . . . "

"Like my meeting with Sandra and those other two agents . . . "

"Precisely. It took every ounce of my being to not actively help you in that moment. I passively threw you some hints that I thought you could handle, and the best I could do was to put Sandra in that room with you." Roger virtually apologized by saying, "I gave you two chances in three that you were going to walk out of there. So good job on that one."

Xantha asked Roger point-blank, "Were you going to take this Program away from me?"

Roger shook his head, "Not after that meeting."

Xantha persisted. "But what if that meeting didn't go the way it did?"

Roger matter-of-factly stated, "The fact that you made it out of that room convinced everyone involved that you were the right person for the job, so to speak. You basically had earned the opportunity to make your case."

Xantha smiled lightly. "Okay. Well, you came here to say what you said. And I hear you. I appreciate the confidence in me and The Program."

Roger stood to leave. "Okay. See you soon."

"Okay."

And then Roger left. And Xantha became wounded, hoping it would simply heal itself. But that was just not her way.

13

Within the confines of funding, The Program laid bare the unspoken truth that, essentially, the budget was bottomless. Or endless. In any case, whatever the economical need that The Program would present, in the end, Xantha would receive whatever she required. More than what she required. Much more. Bottom line, funding was not going to be an issue. And it was time.

The "go date" had been pushed and postponed and delayed for weeks on end, but finally, at long last, the time had come. After months of training that revolved around tactics, weapons, intel, and, to be sure, the ability to remain clandestine, the moment had arrived. But there were a handful of moments that needed to be ironed out.

Roger took point in leading the prototypical group to their first sequence. The target was a serial sexual predator who had been arrested over one hundred times in the last five years and had served only a few months in jail because the people that he targeted were victims that were always reluctant to provide either testimony or evidence. Plus, the laws were just written so poorly that their target simply continued to be released over and over again because authorities could not legally hold him for any length of time. Thomas chose him, authorized the placement of his file into Alpha group's leader's safe deposit box, and distributed the weapons to be used. Roger had taken this group under his wing and had trained them himself at a black site in a friendly southern state, and he felt that they were ready.

Interestingly enough, Roger only needed to instruct these elite soldiers in one tactic. He called it The Wrap. All of these soldiers knew how to execute their targets, but Roger had come up with a finishing move that limited, if not out-and-out eliminated, any physical blowback from their process. One agent would stop the target while two others would approach from behind. The weapon would be placed at the base of the target's head, just under the area where the base of the skull ended, and would be discharged. At the same time, the remaining asset would quickly wrap the head of the target in a towel to prevent and control what was left of the target, and then both would catch the body as it fell, while the primary would hold their legs.

At this point, the cleaning vehicle was already moving into position, and the techs inside were opening the side door to take the target and quickly place him into the simplest of lined pine boxes. The vehicle's door closed and sped to the incinerator previously chosen, leaving the three assets to sweep the scene for any debris that might have been left: a wallet, a watch, a hat. Anything that would have shown that they were ever there. And then the three would drive off separately, back to base. While the vehicle was nearing its destination, someone in the van would redundantly confirm that the proper target was dropped.

Roger would be monitoring through the asset's body cam footage, and only the primary had an earpiece with which to communicate. Roger made it very clear that the less chatter the better. In fact, no talking at all was optimal. And the task should take less than thirty seconds to complete.

As per the protocols set up, the vehicle holding the target sped to the incinerator where the last four operatives would collect the target, place him into the furnace, blast the target, climb into their vehicle, and head back to base. Then the team would simply wait, scouring all media for any trace of the operation for the next forty-eight hours. Should there be no red flags raised, the operation would be deemed a success, and that team would be free to pick up another authorized target at their earliest convenience. It was really going to be that simple. And it was, as this first mission went off without a hitch. The target was acquired, dropped, and incinerated with zero residual forty-eight-hour issues. The time had come to open The Program.

So it came to be that fateful evening where all ten of The Program's groups would be taking their targets at the same time in a three-hour window, and all of it was to be monitored by Roger, Saul, and Xantha. Later, all three would sit down and discuss what went right and what went wrong, correlating it with video footage and the one-page written reports submitted by each primary asset. One by one, each target was being cleanly dropped, neatly wrapped, and whisked to their corresponding endpoints without any issues. Within a ninety-minute time frame, nine out of ten targets had been eliminated. Only one target remained on this opening night, and all eyes became fixed upon it. If this last target could be cleanly dropped on this opening night, there was no telling how far this Program could go.

This last target was becoming a bit of a curve ball. He wasn't where intel said he was going to be, and the Charlie group wasn't entirely sure where he was at that moment. They had a guess, but suppositions and guesses were deemed to be a wild card that had the ability to take this mission down from the inside. There was to be no guessing. Either we knew or we didn't, as Roger would say. And they were approaching the end of their three-hour window. Without notice, the target appeared, but he was entering from the other direction, which placed the weapons in the front, and the primary in the back.

In an impressive feat of improvisation, weapons one closed his gap to his target, raised his piece, and double tapped the heart. As the target fell, the primary caught his shoulder, and the two in front grabbed his feet. The van was late by twenty seconds, which exposed the team for a moment, but no one was about, and they finished their mission, albeit a little backward. Later, as the report would show, there was zero contamination or compromise, and the tenth target was deemed a success.

Once each group had been confirmed to have been safely "done for the day," Xantha, Roger, Saul, and Thomas sat down at the home base to hash out what just happened.

Saul went first. "I think that our opener here was as tight as you could ask. No complaints at all from me."

Thomas agreed. "While not entirely flawless, this was as good as it gets. Tight."

Roger had some tactical issues, such as that last target coming from a different street angle, making his capture longer, but no less flawless than the other nine.

But Xantha raised an interesting point. "Are we confirming our targets only *after* we get them in the vehicle? Where is our initial confirmation coming from?"

Thomas answered. "Well, our initial report comes first from the Department of Defense, which is its own special brand of confirmation. And then the local law enforcement, and then we drop them in the box." Thomas reminded everyone, "As far as both the DOD and the locals are concerned, they're just confirming our request of who and where these criminals are living right now, like a 'Megan's Law' confirmation or something. They have no idea what our parameters are in The Program."

Roger had a thought. "Perhaps we should ask for a dummy list that we have no intention of liquidating. Then, when the DOD or these local yokels see that this list doesn't always have people that we disappear, they'll be satisfied and back off."

Xantha pondered it, then agreed. "Okay. We'll cool it for two weeks right now. Roger will keep quietly training more operatives who can hit the ground running when we crank it up again, but in the meantime, we'll watch the media, reach out to our assets, and just lay low while we compile a tight list that we can act on when the time is right."

Everyone nodded and voiced their approval, and the meeting ended. The Program had begun in earnest, but no one here wanted to become overconfident just yet. They had hit a lead-off homer, but there was still a lot of game left.

Roger immediately went to work reaching out to his friends in high places, and Thomas started to confirm a new list of several hundred targets that were to be deemed "worthy, but safe." Saul had other work to do. Some of the reports from the primaries had indicated that their weapons needed to be discharged twice to be effective, and he was trying to ascertain whether that was a user issue or a weaponry issue. Xantha continued to crunch data, with a long-range outlook as to the feasibility of The Program. She had a hunch that there might be a time limit on this, and she was moving some product and assets to assure her that, when the time inevitably came, she would be protected.

Days became weeks, and then The Program was up and running again, this time with new targets, fuller teams of ten, and a more widespread networking of assets, controlled mostly by Roger and Thomas, with Saul supplying more reliable hardware. Xantha marveled at the meetings she took, and the funding she attained, with virtually no questions asked. The Program, much to her delight, was becoming that which she had always hoped: a wildly effective neutralization program that had yielded so much positive results that no one even thought to look her way.

Someone once said that the days move slowly, but the months and years go fast. Indeed, that was the case with The Program. Xantha had placed a handful of people below each of her primaries, and Thomas, Saul, and Roger had their own set of people who knew nothing at all of what The Program entailed, yet continued to corporately and professionally support them. As far as anyone was concerned, this was just another government program that, unlike all other government programs, was running smoothly and without a hitch.

Data had started to secretly come in as to crime rates, state funding, federal funding, police shootings, arrests, prison population, and how much all of this was costing. Incredibly, just as Xantha had posited all those years ago, all of these numbers were coming way down. Politicians were happy, people were satisfied, and governments, both local and federal, were awash in surplus funds. Taxes were—at worst—stable and—at best—going down. And people who no one would miss were being removed from the equation of civilization. It was all good news, albeit stained with blood, although not the blood of the innocents.

Personally, everyone within The Program was performing well beyond expectations. Privately, some players were beginning to question the morality of eliminating human beings simply because they were costing the rest of us untold amounts of money. But there was something else. And it mostly had to do with Thomas. He had found a sympathetic voice in, of all people, Sandra Gelsig, the woman who was in the room with Xantha, having been placed there by Roger. Sandra began to feel as Thomas did, but her agony was essentially "this was not the mission that I signed up for" mentality, and she was trying to find a way out safely. In the course of human events, Sandra and Thomas would begin to date seriously, which complicated their situation but made each of their lives more tolerable, perhaps the way it is when two famous people find each other.

In any case, as The Program's parameters settled in, eighteen months had passed, and there was nary a whimper from either the media or its citizens whom they informed. Xantha had gathered that the security and competence of The Program had far surpassed anything that anyone would have imagined. Indeed, they had all chosen wisely those that they had recruited to participate.

14

The relationship started innocently enough. Sandra was out by herself at a half-empty bar drowning her sorrows ever so gently, one drink at a time, and in walked on Thomas Duphrane, looking to dull his senses one shot at a time. He couldn't remember the last time he went out, and Sandra couldn't remember the last time she didn't. Two tortured souls meeting at the same time, in the only place they could. By accident.

They noticed each other right away, but neither one knew it. Thomas ordered Scotch and then threw it down and ordered another one. This one he nursed. Only five seats away was Sandra, already well on her way to a good night of drinking, but not so far gone that she didn't want some companionship. *Let the small talk begin,* she thought.

"Rough night?" she asked.

"Rough year," Thomas replied casually, looking in her direction.

They both laughed, and Sandra stepped one chair closer. "What are you drinking?"

"Scotch. Nothing but the best for me."

Sandra stepped closer. "I'll buy you that drink if you come talk to me for a while. I need the company of a stranger tonight."

Thomas was taken aback, but in a good way. Relationships seemed too hard for him lately, and he welcomed one that came gift wrapped.

They talked for some time at the bar without disclosing too much, and then moved to a booth. It was earlier in the night, only being seven o'clock, and they were enjoying each other. Thomas told her he went to the University of Virginia while Sandra said she started in the army right out of high school and thought about seminary, but then went to Maryland and got her law degree. Thomas admitted that he graduated college, but for no good reason. They laughed some more and kept drinking.

As the night went on, Thomas revealed that his father was a pastor, and that seemed to loosen both of them up a little. Certainly, the drinks were helping too, but they clearly had a connection that went beyond the fact that both of them seemed to like each other.

Then Sandra simply blurted something out. "Do you believe in God?"

Thomas laughed at the question, then answered, "Well, *someone* is out to get me, so why not?"

They both laughed at his response, but then Sandra persisted.

"No, really. Are you a believer?"

Thomas really thought about his answer, since, first, he

hadn't thought about it for a while, and second, he didn't want to scare Sandra away. Not yet anyway. "I believe that there is an entity who genuinely cares for us, but, for some reason, that entity also will not stand in our way if we choose to annihilate one another."

Sandra gave a blank look then smiled ever so gently. "Not bad there, Thomas. That's not bad."

That was as deep as the conversation went that evening, and suddenly, it was getting late.

Smiling at each other, they exchanged numbers and promised to see each other again soon. As they both rose to leave, they got one last look at each other. *Not bad*, they both thought. *Not bad at all.*

As Thomas walked home, he thought about his new friend. He liked her very much already, but his lifestyle didn't really have room for love. *Don't worry*, he thought. *This isn't "love," really. It's more of a "like-like."* He promised himself that he would call her in a few days, and then he called her the next night.

Sandra answered after two rings. "Thomas?"

"Sandra?" Thomas waited a beat, fumbled a bit, and asked if she would see him again. She said she would, and they were off.

They met at a bar they both knew, at a time that they knew would be slow, ordered a few drinks, and started to coalesce and gel around each other's words.

Sandra and Thomas ordered some food to pass the time with, followed by a smattering of various drinks to go with it. They talked about their lives and how full they were and then talked some more about their lives and realized how empty they had become.

Thomas began to dig a little deeper. "So you *thought* about seminary? But then . . . "

Sandra smiled. "Yeah, it just didn't take, I guess. I'm a firm believer of either being all-in or all-out. Nothing halfway. Ever." Then she made a joke. "You know what they say? A job half-done is a half-assed job."

Thomas smirked, and then marveled at the simplicity of this girl. "That's not bad," he said. Then he pressed a little farther and harder. "Well, my dad was a pastor, so that's my excuse for not pursuing the cloth. But what's yours? There must be a story here."

Sandra pushed back. "Well, what's *your* story?"

Thomas spoke the truth. "My mother died when I was born, so I went through a good portion of my adolescence thinking I killed my mother."

Sandra's face went a little frigid. She didn't mean to conjure up *that* bad of a memory.

Sensing this, Thomas reassured her. "Oh, don't worry. After years of therapy, and the passage of time, I know that's not true. But it clearly affected me, and through no fault of my own, I became a little distant from God. And a little bit of a fatalist at heart."

Sandra sat silent, then told Thomas *her* story.

"My sister was killed. Randomly. During a botched mugging. And the thing of it was, the guy who mugged her was in and out of jail for his whole life. And some of the stuff that this guy did made me think that they should have locked him up when he was eighteen and just thrown away the key." Sandra's eyes drifted. "I mean, this guy was a child molester, armed robber, and drug addict since forever." She tailed off. "I mean, it was just so stupid and random, and my sister didn't deserve that.

"I mean . . . where was God on that one? Where was the lightning bolt that would have taken this guy away from all of us? This guy seemed just born to hurt people, and that just sucks." Sandra took another sip of her drink then put it down and looked at Thomas.

And he just had this look on his face that just made Sandra know that he completely understood. And in a moment of pure passion, Thomas leaned across their table and kissed Sandra gently on the lips. He stopped kissing her, looked into her eyes, and then they both kissed each other. Hard. And they both thought it was glorious.

They were both wondering if they should stay or go, and they decided to stay awhile longer. Soon, they were holding hands, looking into each other's eyes, telling each other everything. The food and the drinks were forgotten, and the night went on beautifully.

They seemed to be able to see each other every day, and beginning to stay over at each other's places several times a week. Soon, they were a couple in love in a very difficult time for each of them, and then, out of nowhere, their situation became much more complicated.

Sandra had stayed over Thomas's place for the umpteenth time in the three months that they had been together, and, as couples do, she began to playfully snoop around his apartment while Thomas was in the shower. She went into his closet and smelled his clothes. She casually looked under his bed and found nothing of note. She opened his top dresser drawer and found a box with change in it. She lightheartedly thought about taking four quarters and then giving them back to him the next time they went to dinner. She placed her hand in the box and realized it had a false bottom. Intrigued, she lifted the top out, and found something underneath that she recognized.

It was a safe deposit box key, but this was no ordinary key. This one had no number on it, and it was made of an alloy of some kind. And then Sandra turned it over and saw a stamp. A stamp that she had on *her* safe deposit box key. For *her* safe deposit box. For The Program.

A shot of terror went through her body. Was Thomas the same as her? A soldier in The Program? *No . . . impossible*, she thought. But she couldn't shake it, and she had to get it together before Thomas came out of the shower. She wanted to leave, but she loved him. She wanted to stay, but she was so afraid. Paralyzed by fear, love, and a thirst to know the truth, Sandra just stood in the middle of the room. Wearing Thomas's robe, she held out the key for him to see as he emerged from the steam-filled shower room. He was wearing one towel around his waist and drying his hair with another. She felt a tear begin to run down her face. The tear was one of sadness, fear, and relief all at once. She held out the key. And she waited for him to see.

Thomas was drying his hair and was walking toward Sandra. He was smiling, then he saw the key in her hand, and he wasn't. Calmly, but with purpose, he asked her, "Where did you find that?"

She didn't answer, and her breathing became shallow.

Thomas asked again. "Where did you find that?" He was moving closer to Sandra now, as she simply held out the key.

Finally, she looked to her right, and then Thomas did too. He saw the open box, and then he knew.

Thomas shrugged. "It's just a key to my safe deposit box. That's all." He was still confused as to why Sandra was so affected, and he was also unsure about how he should react. "What's wrong, Sandra?"

Sandra dropped her arm, his key still in hand, and walked over to her purse. She rifled through it, unzipped a pocket, and pulled out *her* key. It was the same as Thomas's: alloy in structure, no number, and a stamp on the reverse. She then held Thomas's key up in one hand and hers in the other. Identical. Almost the same. This very special key. One they only give to special people who enjoy special privileges. Then, Sandra spoke.

"Who do you work for?"

Thomas thought, then replied, "I work for the government. I told you that."

"*No!*" She yelled. "Who! What's the name of your boss! Who do you report to?"

Thomas was taken aback. He didn't know what the right answer was or why she was asking. Where was she going with this?

"I know what *my* key opens," Sandra continued, "so now I'm asking you what *your* key opens."

Thomas held up his hands in a "whoa whoa whoa" behavior, then he spoke. "Sandra, why are you so angry?"

Sandra answered.

"Because this key is the key to something that I can't do anymore. It has funded and authorized and breathed life into something that I can't even *believe* that I am a part of. Everything about what this key represents can be summed up in one word: *murder!* State-sanctioned, government-funded, cold-blooded murder! I thought I was on the right side of vengeance, but now, I've since realized that I'm on the wrong side! I have been trying to get out, trying to save

myself, desperate to save my own soul, but I know now . . .
I'm trapped in this thing forever. I know this, but I was hoping, *praying*, that maybe I've finally found someone worth
living for!" She started to sob. "And now I find *this*? On *you*!
And you are a part of this abomination too?" She collapsed
on the bed, sitting on its edge, and started to whisper. "Oh
my God, oh my God. What is happening here? Oh my God."
Then she snapped to, and stood up again.

"Who do you work for?" Thomas spoke slowly, but delib-
erately. "I'm going to tell you. Right now. It's going to be okay.
Just relax Sandra. I need you to relax. Can you do that? For me?"

Sandra thought about it, then nodded. "Okay. The person
I work for is named Xantha Grasso. Does that name mean
anything to you?"

Sandra's eyes grew wide, and then she answered. "Yes. I
know Xantha. I had a chance to kill her once, and I should
have done it too, but Roger told me not to."

Thomas looked at her quizzically. "When was this?"

"I was alone in a room with her a long time ago, when
all this was just beginning. Two other lower-level operatives
were with me at the time, and I was instructed to observe
and assist. Roger said if that meeting went sideways, that
I was to eliminate those operatives, and then take Xantha
to meet Roger. But that didn't happen, and I stood down."

Thomas was trying to figure out where and when that
could have been, but then shook his head and abandoned
that train of thought. It went nowhere, and he knew he
was never going to figure that out. Not now anyway. Then
Thomas asked, "So Roger is *your* boss?"

Sandra nodded. "Since the beginning, he's been the one
that I have been taking orders from."

Thomas then took the opportunity to calm this situation down and lay out to Sandra what he had planned. "Sandra. You're not going to believe this, but I want what you want, and for the exact same reason. The Program *is* state-sanctioned murder and for a time, I just looked the other way. But I have completely lost my taste for it now, and I am looking to get out too. Maybe . . . maybe we can help each other do that."

Then, Thomas continued.

"You're not going to like this, but this Program was something that I helped bring about. I'm one of the founding members on some level."

"How's that?" Sandra asked.

"Well," Thomas continued, "I'm the one who initially chose the targets. I drew up those plans, and I submitted them to both Roger and Xantha, and those plans were approved. So a lot of this is my fault."

Sandra stood silent then sat down. She didn't seem to care too much about that aspect. But she became eager to hear what Thomas's plan was to somehow extract both himself and Sandra from this Program, so she spoke one last time.

"What are we going to do?"

Thomas shook his head. "I'm not sure. I have an idea, but we'll think of something together, I promise." Then Thomas added, "And I don't even care anymore what happens to me. I just can't do this any longer."

It was all quiet now as Sandra calmed down, and Thomas fell deeper in love.

Then both of them climbed into bed together and held each other tight. They hardly spoke at all before they both drifted off to sleep. There was worry here, but for the first time in a long while, there was also relief. Both of them were closer to the end of this ordeal than they could ever realize at that moment. And they dreamed the dream of the righteous and slept as they hadn't slept in years.

When they awoke, Sandra and Thomas showered together for safety's sake and began to make their plans. They did not want to talk on the phone, and they were wary of their cars and apartments right now. Thomas reminded Sandra that within the rooms at the banks, where the safe deposit boxes are kept, there can be no surveillance by law. They agreed to speak to each other about how to leave The Program only when they were there. They moved quietly about their lives, continuing to do their jobs as required. Wednesday and Friday, for the next three weeks, they would meet in various bank rooms, as they discussed their escape.

"I need to blow this Program wide open," Thomas would say, "and I have a friend at the *Daily Chronicle* who's a reporter who would love this story."

"Can you trust her?" Sandra asked.

"I think so," said Thomas. "I went to college with her. Her name is Jen. I doubt she even remembers me. But I always had her number in my back pocket, just in case I needed it."

"I just hope the number still works."

Thomas was keenly aware how much Xantha valued her privacy, both personally and professionally, and Thomas going to the press about The Program was something that Xantha was simply not going to tolerate. This had to be done just right. But even the best laid plans can fall apart quickly if not carried out to the letter, as Thomas and Sandra were about to learn. Their world had become just too small . . .

15

Sandra and Thomas awoke to a new day several weeks later. The sun was just a little warmer, and the air was just a little crisper. They had both revealed to each other how they had sat in the darkness, and now looked to move into the light. This really was the first day of the rest of their lives.

As they both rose from their slumber, Thomas's cell phone buzzed from a number he didn't recognize. He answered and found out that it was the hospital. Thomas's father, Pastor Jeff, had been admitted the previous evening. He had complained about nausea followed by a bout of vomiting and then some soreness of his gut. When they examined Pastor Jeff, they realized there was something much more serious than gastrointestinal distress, and they held him for observation overnight.

Running some tests, the doctor revealed over the phone that Thomas's father had stage four pancreatic cancer. He was not going to live more than a few more weeks, so Pastor

Jeff had instructed the doctor to call Thomas and have him come in as soon as he could. Thomas told the doctor that he would be there sometime that day, and he hung up.

Stunned by this turn of events, he turned to Sandra and simply said, "My father is dying. I'm going to have to go see him later today."

Sandra nodded, said that she was sorry, and promised to wait here for him until he returned from his visit. She was exhausted anyway and could use the rest.

Thomas had an embarrassingly detached relationship with his father. He should have spent more time with him, as all sons feel they should, and now he wanted nothing more than to be with him at the end of his life. He had always been sorry for not having a stronger relationship with his dad and had no excuse for this lapse. Monday became Tuesday, and then Wednesday moved into Friday, and then Saturday could wait, while Sunday would be too late. It was an all too familiar equation throughout the history of time, this father-son relationship, and Thomas was genuinely sorry for this. But he was here now, and he left to visit his father in the hospital.

As Thomas arrived, he asked the front desk where his father was being kept.

"Fifth floor, room 123. Oncology. He's up there now."

Thomas thanked her and made his way up. As he exited the elevator, he made a right turn, and saw that his father's room was at the end of the hall, isolated from all the others. His dad had a single room, and he was all alone. As he made his way down the hall, he saw his dad turn his head, and he smiled.

"Just follow the wires, son," he joked, and that made Thomas smile as well.

Reaching his dad's room, Thomas pulled up a chair next to the bed, and sat down. "Hello, father."

"Hello, son."

Then, Thomas asked a stupid question. "How are you?"

Pastor Jeff laughed. "I'm certain that I've been better, but I'm sure that I've been worse as well."

Thomas marveled at his father's cavalier attitude toward his impending death, but then again, his dad *was* a pastor.

Then his father sighed and proclaimed that he would soon be with his mother in paradise, so it was not *all* bad. "They gave me something for the pain, so I feel pretty good actually."

Thomas smiled affectionately and nodded.

In the way only a father could, Pastor Jeff looked at his son and surmised a dilemma. "What's wrong, son?"

Thomas, who had only told his dad that he worked for the government, just shrugged. "Nothing, sir. Just . . . a lot on my mind."

His dad nodded back with a knowing look. They sat in silence for a while, Thomas admiring his father's strength, his father worrying about his son. "Don't worry about me, son. I am more than ready to meet my maker. On some level, I'm relieved. I know what's wrong with me, and I know my time is short. I have more information than most people do at the end of their life."

Thomas smiled again, and then a tear fell down his cheek as his eyes welled up. "Dad? I need to ask you something, and I'm sorry that I'm making you work right now."

"Think nothing of it, Thomas. I'm always ready, willing, and able to talk shop with you. Frankly, it's all I have left."

Thomas paused for a moment, took a breath, and spoke.

"Are you saved, dad?"

His father smiled at his son and said, "Isn't that my line?"

Thomas continued, "But how do you know?"

Pastor Jeff could see that this was no ordinary question from Thomas, so he answered as a man of the cloth would. "I know that Jesus Christ is my Lord and Savior, and I have sacrificed my life to him long ago. Whatever the definition of 'salvation' is, I'm comfortable that I have been moving in that direction for my entire life."

Pastor Jeff continued, "Now, am I perfect? Far from it. Am I flawed? Absolutely. Am I good enough to have the privilege of arriving at the feet of the Son of Man who sits at the right hand of God? Almost certainly no. But that is why I need Jesus. That is why we *all* need Jesus. He saves those who are unworthy. Whatever your sin may be, your salvation is nigh. And he does this all in the name of love. All one needs to do is ask for His forgiveness, and his Grace shall be laid over you."

Thomas, clearly impressed, was nonetheless skeptical. "I'm afraid, Dad. I'm afraid for my friends, and I'm afraid for me. I mean . . . how can what you say be true? How can that be?"

Pastor Jeff looked at his son, and he saw his son more lost and afraid than he had ever seen him before. Thomas had an almost pathetic look of sadness and despair that Pastor Jeff had seen many times on others, but never on Thomas. This look concerned him greatly, and he therefore looked to put Thomas at ease in the only way he knew how. He told a story. "Thomas," Pastor Jeff began, "I'm going to tell you something, and I really need you to listen."

Thomas, through eyes full of tears, nodded desperately and listened.

"When I was in seminary, I always remarked to myself

how fortunate I was to have the instructors that I did. Even at that point, I knew that I was surrounded by both greatness and great people. Some of my professors went on to have long, illustrious careers serving God. Many were able to advance deep into the church's hierarchy, making policy, tackling issues, and making a real difference both within the church and without.

"One of these men was Professor O'Neill, who would go on to become a bishop on the East Coast in one of the largest districts in this country. I always lamented never having him as an instructor, and I always saw him on campus from a distance. One day, as I was going to the campus library, I saw him coming down the stairs toward me all alone. His robes were gently flapping as he strode, and he held a Bible in his one hand as he held onto his hat with the other. For me, it was akin to seeing Zeus . . .

"In any case, as he turned to move past me, he stepped onto a patch of ice, slipped, and did the most gracious pratfall that you could ever imagine. I went to help him up, but he had already bounced to his feet, no worse for wear, and he thanked me for the help up and went on his way. I was more embarrassed than he was, I'm sure. Then, my eyes moved to the statue that was casting the shadow. There were two statues, actually. One was the one of Blind Justice holding her two scales, and the other was a replica of the Christ the Redeemer statue that you can find in the country of Brazil." Moving toward his crescendo, Pastor Jeff paused to make certain that Thomas was listening and was also paying attention.

"The shadows that both statues cast were coming from the two symbols that served as the lynchpins of not only my degrees of study, but also of civilization itself: justice and faith. And within those shadows lies a darkness of some kind. It is cold there, the sun does not shine, and it's not even the same shape, but the shadows *are* connected somehow, and that is as close as we are ever going to get. It's important that you understand this, Thomas. Do you understand?"

Thomas nodded. "Yes. That sometimes justice and faith are simply not the same here on Earth as it is in heaven."

Pastor Jeff was pleased. "That's right, son. Not now, not ever. They are never the same. But, within the confines of this world, it's as close as we get." He then reached out for his son's hand, and grasped it firmly, "And that is just going to have to be okay."

Thomas understood, and put his other hand over top of his father's.

His father then ended with this.

"I can tell that you are hurting, son, and I can only say this. Get yourself right with God. Don't be the man who flees his burning house with his hair singed. Don't be the man who is forever separated from God by an insurmountable chasm because you have waited too long." Pastor Jeff smiled, and then patted his son's hand. "Trust yourself to do the right thing, and everything will be fine."

Thomas, tears falling down his cheeks, rose to leave. "I have to go, Dad."

His father smiled and replied, "So do I."

Thomas kissed his father on the forehead, turned, and left. He did not look back, and he entered the elevator to leave. As he stood in the elevator, Thomas pulled out his phone. He scrolled through his contacts and found the one marked "Jen Reporter" and began to dial. Jen, *not* Jenn. *She hates that*, he remembered.

The call connected, and Thomas heard, "*Daily Chronicle*, this is Jen."

"Jen. This is Thomas Duphrane. Do you remember me?"

"Yes, you called me a few weeks ago. How are you? What's up? I haven't heard from you since that day where you said you had a 'big story' or something."

"I'm ready to tell you. A story of all stories, no kidding."

Jen was silent then asked, "Okay. What is it?"

Thomas answered. "I can't tell you on the phone right now. Can I call you later?"

"Sure. What time?"

"I can call you tomorrow around 7:00 a.m.," Thomas replied.

"Okay," Jen said. "Tomorrow. I look forward to it."

As Jen hung up, she scrolled through her own address book and found a number that she had been given only one month earlier. She marked it "Ghost," tapped it, and then dialed.

A man picked up at the other end. "Yes?"

Jen replied, "Go secure." Jen heard a click and a squelch.

A voice said, "Go ahead, you are secure."

"It's me. That thing that you told me might happen? It's happening tomorrow at 7:00 a.m."

"You're sure it's him? Thomas Duphrane?" the voice said.

"Yes. It was him."

"Good work," the voice said. "I'll take it from here. And do yourself a favor. Delete this number, and forget you ever called it. Ever."

The line clicked, and it was over.

16

It was on the news . . .

And it seemed to be meant to get Xantha's attention.

"In other news today, a small unidentified revolutionary force has removed the terrorist leader Robert Katanga from his post in the African nation of Rwanda." A wave of panic, then rage ran through Xantha's body, and at the same time, a chill went down her spine. She knew what was coming next.

"The Rwandan leader was last seen in the city of Kigali only one week ago, but he has not resurfaced since his ouster. The White House has no comment on the matter. In a statement, the Rwandan government hopes to be able to restore diplomatic relations with the United States sooner than later, and will accept any assistance the US might provide as their new government takes shape."

Xantha was stunned. Was this really happening? There was no way that her team was going to be exposed by this half-wit in the White House, was there? Just as she was reaching for her phone, it rang. It was Roger.

Xantha picked it up. "Roger?" Silence. "Roger?" she asked again.

This time, Roger answered, but it seemed like he was being careful as to what he was going to say. "The president has requested a meeting with us. Can you be ready in an hour? We'll pick you up."

"We'll? Who's 'we'?"

"Don't worry about that. Be ready in an hour. Bring your phone, ID, and yourself. That's it."

Click.

Xantha wasn't worried for her life, but she *was* worried about her Program. She was glad that she was only going to have to wait an hour for her answer as to what was going on. She had a guess, but nothing could really prepare her for what was really happening.

A car was waiting forty-five minutes later, and Xantha climbed inside. Roger was there, as was Saul. Quickly, they were whisked away. Just those three and the driver, with his single red light on the dashboard clearing traffic. Within forty minutes, they were at the gates of the White House, and they flashed their IDs and drove up front. It was about 7:00 p.m. on a Friday, and no one was around but security. They were ushered into the Oval Office, where they waited, presumably for the president. After five minutes, President Crumb appeared, and the room was cleared of everyone but two Secret Service agents, Roger, Saul, and Xantha. Then the president spoke.

"I want you to know that I admire your work. And I'm not the only one. Let's get right to it. I used your Charlie team to take out the dictator Robert Katanga, and they completed their mission as only your team can."

Xantha knew what that meant. Katanga was gone, and no one was going to find him.

President Crumb moved toward Xantha to speak. "Is there anything you want to say to me?"

Xantha took a breath, looked at Roger, and then spoke calmly. "Are you taking my Program away from me?"

The president laughed. "Not at all. I also admire your tenacity as to the ownership of your team. No, I am not taking your Program away from you." Then, he leaned in and whispered, "I could, but I don't do that to people who are on the same side as I am. Never have, never will."

Xantha then asked another question. "Then why am I here?" The two agents left the room, and now it was just Roger, Saul, Xantha, and the president. The president put his hand on her shoulder, squeezing it gently but firmly. "Because you have a problem."

Saul squirmed a bit as the president looked at both him and Roger. "You can tell her, Agent Vitetto."

Saul took a deep breath, sighed, and then spoke. "It's Agent Duphrane. He's compromised. So is Sandra. They're trying to get out, and they went to the press through our contact at the *Chronicle*. You know her. Jen, the one with all the hair. I got to her first, so luckily, it didn't go any farther than that."

Xantha didn't understand. "What? How? Why?"

Then Saul hit Xantha with a bombshell. "I suspected they were unhappy, so I bugged their phones. Nothing. I bugged his and her place. Nothing. Then, I thought about it . . . and bugged the banks. All ten of them. I figured they might talk in the safe deposit room, and they did. For the last three weeks. They met multiple times, talked about getting out and exposing us all. And The Program."

The president chimed in. "Now, we can't have that, can we? I mean, The Program is working. Your Program is working. Better than anyone *ever* thought it would. You chose the right people, made the right decisions, and brilliantly made all the right moves." The president then spoke plainly. "You sidestepped every landmine that was out there, and now here you are, one step away from greatness. Deputy Director . . . "

Xantha looked at the president, then at Roger, who nodded. Saul also shot her a knowing grin. "Yes, Agent Grasso. A permanent position in a newly formed agency. The Department of Domestic Security."

Xantha smiled broadly, then her smile fell. "What do I need to do?" she asked naively.

"Agent Thomas Duphrane. I'm going to have to ask you to bring him in. In your own special way, using your own team, I'm going to allow you to deal with him in the way that only you can." Xantha was more okay with this than she thought she would be, and a type of calm fell over her. She shot a glance at Saul.

He nodded.

"I'll get him out. I know exactly where he is. He's as good as caught," Roger agreed. "He doesn't know that we know, but that won't hold." Roger looked at Saul. "We should go now. Time is of the essence." Then Roger spoke to Xantha. "We'll bring him to you at the place you like. Saul's room. You know which one I mean?"

Xantha nodded.

"Okay, Saul, let's go."

The two agents who had left the room reappeared and escorted Saul and Roger out. And then Saul and Roger were gone. And it was just Xantha and the president.

"There is one other thing that I need from you," the president remarked. Then he went and sat at his desk, leaving Xantha standing in front of it. Crumb then laid it all out for her. "Here's the thing, Agent Grasso. I like you. I like how you think. I happen to think the same way you do, and that's to everyone's advantage."

Xantha waited for the rest of it.

Then the president spoke again. "I'm going to pass a law. It's on the edge, controversial. But I know a lot of senators and my constituents all seem to feel the same way." He waited for her full attention, then spoke again. "I'm going to give every family, every individual, every taxpayer a five-thousand-dollar write-off . . . for *not* having a child. For the next two years. If you don't have a child, then you get the write-off."

Xantha was unmoved, but she understood. "So, Mr. President. You're rewarding people for *not* reproducing."

Crumb nodded, "Yes. We're going to have to work it out, of course, and there are going to be lawsuits galore, plus an enormous amount of pushback all around." Then he finished, "But I don't care. It passes. It doesn't pass. It doesn't matter to me. Because it's just interference for you. I'm going to raise a bunch of issues, get people all riled up, make them look at me or over here . . ." and he motioned with his hands, "and over there."

"And up here . . . and down there. And the people won't know what hit them. And you can keep doing what you are doing. And no one will be the wiser."

And then he and Xantha said the same thing at the same time. "Kansas City Shuffle . . . "

The president smiled and nodded. "That's right . . . "

Xantha was satisfied. "Okay, sir. You got it. I help you, you look the other way. And we keep moving forward."

"And Thomas goes."

"And Thomas goes," Xantha agreed.

Then, against her better judgment, Xantha stepped forward and spoke out of turn. She was still enraged about the use of her team without her knowledge. She still didn't think that the president realized how close he came to exposing everything: her, The Program, Roger, and anyone and everyone who was working toward the greater good by executing her Program. She had sacrificed everything, creating her pillar of greatness, and now she was going to sacrifice one of her dearest friends who had just become one of her gravest enemies, and it was all on the president's say so. So she took her one last shot at the leader of the free world, and then it would be over.

"Mr. President. Don't you ever use my team this way again without my authorization, do you understand me? I want you to know that I want what you want. I want this thing to run right. But if you ever expose me and my team like this again, well . . . it won't be *my* face you see last. And trust me on this: my word counts."

The president smirked behind his desk.

Xantha finished, "I need you to say that you understand, so that there are no mistakes. Do you understand?"

The president hesitated, thought about it, and then answered. "I've been so advised."

Then he got in his parting shot. "But know this. Just in

case you have forgotten, I *am* the president of the United States. Don't you ever threaten me again, or I will visit it back on you tenfold. People you know and care about will begin to disappear. Their bodies will not be found. You will suffer in such a way that you will wish that you were dead, and then I will personally *grant* that wish. Is *that* in any way unclear?"

Reading the room perfectly, Xantha answered. "I've been so advised."

Then, in a selfless act of both enormous courage and tremendous balls, Xantha strode forward, hand extended.

The president stood up, marveling at her gesture and extended his hand and shook hers. The deal with the devil was done and, miraculously, there was only victory here. No defeats. A rare moment in a unique day that dictated the future of both parties. And both futures were bright.

About the Author

Christopher Graham is lifetime resident of Hunterdon County, New Jersey, and *The Program* is his debut novel. A graduate of Thomas Edison State College, Christopher has spent the last ten years studying both domestic and international history, as his book enthusiastically reflects.

Christopher lives and works out of his home in High Bridge with his loving wife, Sandra. At the time of publication, Christopher is running for local office as a councilman. He can often be found reading a book about American history on his front porch.

Christopher loves cooking, his cat, and writing ever since he was the feature writer of his school newspaper.

LORI,

ENJOY THE

BOOK!

CHG